"Having gifts that differ according to the grace given us, let us use them."

Romans 12:6

# PROLOGUE

"You boys think you know everything there is to know, don't ya?"

The four of us turned our heads to see who was speaking. The late afternoon sun dropping over the football field, where we'd just finished practice, forced us to put our hands over our eyes to see that familiar face. The same face that always seemed to have a huge smile connected to it. We didn't know that moment would change our lives in ways that we could never imagine.

It was Walter Harlow, the school's maintenance man. But all the students, and pretty much all the faculty, just called him "Harley." He'd been working there for way longer than any of us had even thought about being alive.

David was the first one to ask the question we were all wondering. "Are you talking to us, Harley?"

He laughed softly before answering, "I believe I am."

I guess since David was the one to ask the question, he felt it was his place to continue. "What do you mean that we think we know everything there is to know?"

"Well, you're all seniors," Harley answered. "In another year you'll be in college. Then in four more years you'll be out in the real world. So I'm sure you think you've got it all figured out."

"You mean we don't?" Will, always the sarcastic one, asked.

Harley laughed a little bit harder and said, "Not even close, boys. Not even close."

"So what do we need to know?" Will asked him, this time keeping his sarcasm in check.

"Oh, y'all might be getting a good education," Harley continued. "You're not at one of the finest boarding schools in the country for nothing. You probably make good grades and write some really nice papers for your classes. I bet all of you will get great SAT scores too. But do you know anything about life? The kind of stuff that will get you a whole lot further in the world than any grades or SAT scores ever will?"

Will's sarcasm quickly came back as he said, "That depends on exactly what you're talking about."

"Do y'all really want to know?" Harley asked. "Because I can tell you."

"Tell us, please," Brewer begged.

Harley rolled his eyes and smirked. "Oh, you think it's something I can tell you right here in just a few minutes? No, sir, it's gonna take a lot longer than that."

"How long?" Brewer asked.

"How does all year sound?" Harley replied.

"Huh, all year?" I asked, thinking I may have heard him wrong.

I had barely finished my question before he jumped in with his answer. "That's right, all year. But not every day. We've still got eight and a half months of school left, so I figure I can set you boys straight AND get you started on the right path if we meet once a week."

"Meet?" David seemed confused. "Where? When?"

Harley looked around before responding, "How about right here? On the hill overlooking the football field. You'll be down there practicing every afternoon, anyway. So after practice, meet me up here. Every Monday."

"Are you serious?" Will wanted to know.

"I don't bother wasting my time saying stuff I don't mean," Harley said. "Yes, I'm serious. But don't worry, I won't keep you long. You'll have plenty of time to get a shower before dinner."

As he walked away we all looked at each other. Not only were we confused, but it was maybe the first time

I'd seen the four of us all completely silent. Then Harley looked over his shoulder and hollered back at us. "Oh, by the way. What you'll learn from me will be a lot more valuable than anything you'll learn in any classroom on this campus. Just don't go telling anybody I said that."

# CHAPTER ONE

Normally when we got back to our dorm after practice we headed straight to the showers. But this time we went into Brewer's room, simply because it was the first one that we got to.

Brewer was the middle name of Thomas Brewer, obviously a family name, and the one he went by. It was the maiden name of his great-grandmother, but we usually just called him "Brew." He was maybe three inches taller than I was, which isn't much to brag about, and had jet black hair. He came from very old Virginia money and had impeccable manners, calling everybody over the age of twenty "Sir" and "Ma'am." His father was a congressman for three terms. Before that his grandfather was a United States senator for four terms. But like most people that come from that kind of background, he never spoke of it. I'm not even sure if he knew that we knew.

He sat on the corner of his desk before asking what we were all thinking, "What was that?"

"You tell me," David answered. David was from Maryland. Though we had students from more than half the states and several countries, the majority were from Maryland, D.C., Virginia and North Carolina. He had curly dark blonde hair and was probably close to a foot taller than I was. He wasn't on the cross country team but ran as much as any of the guys who were. That would explain his thin frame. He was not exactly quiet, but compared to the rest of us he was. I'll just say he was sort of reserved. At times shy. But if you got him going, he could talk the ears off a statue. All the students at the nearby girls schools, that we regularly had functions with, thought he was good looking. But he didn't seem to notice.

Each room on campus held two students and had a long desk designed for both. There was a shelf going across the top of the desk with a divider to separate each person's books. Below that was a wall that every boy had covered with pictures of friends and family from back home. Most rooms had bunk beds. But this one, being in the senior dorm, had twin beds. One on each wall. Those walls were lined with posters of expensive cars we hoped to one day drive, athletes we admired, and super models we wished we could date. Some posters were from our favorite movies. Brewer's room was no different.

Will had plopped down in one of the chairs at the desk in Brewer's room. He was from Alabama. One of several kids from the deep south. He usually had to barely open his mouth before that thick accent came across his lips. And what did come across those lips was often a wisenheimer comment. He was also tall, though not like David, and had a very athletic build. His hair was so blonde you could almost call it white.

"In all my years being here," he said, "I think that's the most I've ever heard Harley talk. Usually he just kinda nods and says, 'Hey' as he passes."

"What are we going to do?' Brewer asked.

"I don't know," Will continued. "It's not like we're going to get in trouble if we don't meet with him."

"Maybe not," I said. "But I am kinda curious to see what he wants to tell us. Aren't y'all?"

"I am," said David.

Will leaned back in his chair and said, "I guess I am too."

Brewer agreed. "Yeah, it's so weird."

"So we're all agreed we'll give it a try?" I asked.

"Yep," Brewer said.

Will nodded his head and said, "Why not? It'll probably be more interesting than some of classes we sit through. Even Harley said something like that."

"Sounds good to me," David said as he headed to the door. "But we'd better hurry or we'll be late for dinner."

## CHAPTER TWO

The Dowling School was one of the many boarding schools on the east coast, and one of several in Virginia. It was named for the Dowling family who had at one point owned all the land where the school is. But that was a long time ago. The school was now 185 years old.

It wasn't much different than many of the other boarding schools around except for one thing. It was right on the river. That may not sound like a big deal, but when you were walking from one class to another, or heading back to your dorm, seeing that view was pretty cool. Especially in the early morning when the fog was rising up from it.

"Dowling," as it was simply known, was still an all boys school. There was talk a few years before I arrived of making it coed. Many other boys schools had done that. But the board of directors voted against it. I guess for tradition, I'm not really sure. But we had some sort of function with one of the local girls schools almost every weekend. Usually a dance or sometimes a day trip to an amusement park. Occasionally even to Washington or Baltimore for a sporting event.

While all the boarding schools in Virginia were our rivals in sports, even the ones that weren't in our conference, we didn't "hate" them like college rivals do. Probably because almost every kid at a Virginia boarding school had strongly considered going to some of the others. I would really come to understand that as an adult. Whenever I met someone who went to one of our rival schools, there was an instant bonding. We would always know some of the same people, even if we were several years apart in age.

The four of us had been good friends since our freshman year. We were all on the same hall of the freshman dorm, though none of us were roommates. Come to think of it, even though we were always on the same floor of the same dorm, none of us ever lived together. Maybe that was why we all got along so well.

Oh, my name is Ben. I grew up in a small town in eastern North Carolina that you've probably never even heard of, much less visited. I don't know how to describe how I was back then. I was decent at every sport I played, but hardly very athletic. I was a good student, but there was no chance I'd be the valedictorian. I was not the funny one like Will or the one the girls loved like David. Nor was I the rich one like Brewer. But somehow, I managed to fit in. I guess I'm good at noticing and remembering everything. Maybe that's why I'm the one telling this story.

## CHAPTER THREE

The next Monday came along pretty quickly. We hadn't mentioned our meeting with Harley since we first talked about it in Brewer's room almost a week earlier. We still weren't even sure if he was serious. But as we walked off the football field from practice, we looked up to the top of the hill where he'd said to meet. Sure enough, he was there.

As we started the not so long, but sometimes tough after a practice, walk up the hill, he yelled down to us. "I bet y'all weren't sure if I'd actually be here or not, were you? Well, here I am, and right on time. I was born three days late and I was really embarrassed about it, so I've never been late for anything since."

It was hard not to laugh, and we all did, just as we got to the top of the hill overlooking the football field and the river. Harley sat down on a big rock that was half buried into the ground. "Grab some ground, boys," he told us. So we all sat down on the grass facing him.

He took off his cap with the Dowling logo and rubbed his nearly bald head before putting it back on. He seemed to have several Dowling caps with the various orange and blue school colors, and he was always wearing one. But never indoors. Even if he was just walking in a building for a quick moment, he removed it. Usually a few seconds before he walked inside somewhere, just to play it safe.

There was a nice breeze coming off the river which we hadn't felt down on the football field. Harley looked down in that direction before he said, "That's quite a view, isn't it?" We all looked to our right and nodded in agreement. Then he continued. "Don't take that view for granted, because you won't always have it. There's no telling how many thousands of boys have looked down at that river over the last hundred and eighty five years and not realized how lucky they were to get to see it. Several times a day, at that. One day you'll be working in some big city and you won't have that river to look at every day. Then you'll start to realize just how lucky you were."

Then Harley slapped the rock he was sitting on with the palm of his hand. "See this rock?" he asked. "It's probably something else you take for granted. But this rock has probably been here since before this land became your school. It's probably even older than I am."

We all giggled a little bit. Harley couldn't help but laugh too. His round, dark face behind a solid white beard made him seem heavier than he was. He was in pretty good shape, though. Not very tall, but solid. He had a contagious laugh that I guess none of us had ever noticed. It made us laugh even harder.

Several seconds later he stopped laughing, and we did too. Then he paused for a moment before smacking the rock again. "Just imagine what this rock has been through. How many boys have sat on it. No telling how many of y'all I've seen sitting here studying or reading. I've even seen a few people trying to draw pictures of the view. Some better than others. But just like the view, this rock is something you'll probably take for granted in your four years here. Then you'll miss it."

"Miss a rock?" Will asked.

"Yep. You'll be surprised," Harley answered. "And that leads me to my point for today. Does it seem like more than three years ago that y'all first got here to Dowling?"

"It barely seems like one," Brewer said.

Harley pointed to him as he rose a few inches off the rock. "Exactly!" he said. "And a few years from now it will still seem like it was just one year ago. Because time flies. And the older you get, the quicker it seems to fly. If you think your years here go by fast, just wait until you get older. Your college years will go by even quicker. Then the next thing you know you'll be thirty and wondering where your twenties went. Your thirties and forties are gonna go by even faster. Then all of a sudden, you'll be seventy and asking yourself where your life has gone."

We all looked around at each other to see our different reactions. Then we looked back at him to see what he had to say next.

"Boys, life is short, and it moves fast to make it even shorter," Harley said. "That's why you can't waste a single moment of it. All of you probably have big dreams and things you want to accomplish. Everybody does. But the reason most people don't accomplish what they always thought they would is because they get caught in a bad case of the somedays."

Brew seemed puzzled and slightly raised his hand as if he were in class. "The Sundays?" he asked.

Harley grinned. "Not the Sundays," he answered. "The SOMEDAYS."

"What's that mean?" I asked him.

"It means that everybody says they'll do everything they set out to do…someday," Harley replied. "'Someday I'll go to Europe. Someday I'll start my own business. Someday I'll run a marathon. Someday I'll do this. Someday I'll do that.' Then before you know it, someday has come and gone and you haven't done anything you wanted to do."

"Why?" Brew asked, only this time without raising his hand.

"I'm glad you asked, young man," Harley said. "I'll tell you why. It's because they're talked out of it."

"Who talks them out of it?" Brewer wanted to know.

"Do you really want to know?" Harley asked.

Brewer nodded his head before Harley went on. "People talk THEMSELVES out of it."

"They do?" Will said.

"Sad, isn't it?" Harley answered. "But that's right. People talk themselves out of doing what they want to do. Yep, they'll look for any excuse. 'I'm too young. I'm too old. It's too soon. It's too late. I'm too inexperienced. I'm too this. I'm too that.' Then, like I said, someday is here and they've given up on everything. People spend the first half of their lives saying it's too soon. Then they spend the second half of their lives saying it's too late. In fact, if you think about it, what do the first letters in each word of talked out of spell?"

"Talked out of? T-O-O," Will answered.

"Yeah," Harley said. "But what's that spell?"

"Too," David and I said together.

Harley slapped his hands together. "Exactly!" he almost shouted. "Too. Too means *Talked Out Of*. People use the excuse of too everything so much, that they talk themselves out of everything."

We all nodded our heads understanding. Harley nodded his as well. "I'm glad y'all understand me," he said. "Now just don't go through life saying too, because if you do, everything will be talked out of."

"And another thing," he continued. "Don't put your dreams off….START!"

"Start what?" Brewer asked.

"That's for you to decide, not me," Harley said. "But whatever it is you want to do, start it. Like I was saying a minute ago, so many people think they've got plenty of time. Then, all of a sudden, their opportunity has passed them by. That's why I say start."

He looked down at us, then asked, "How do you spell start?"

"Is this a trick question?" Will asked underneath a smirk.

Harley squinted his eyes over at him. "Trick questions are only for people who don't know the answer," he said. "Now come on, it's not that hard. How do you spell start?"

David and Brewer chimed in, "S-T-A-R-T."

"Are we missing something?" I asked.

"Just my point," Harley answered. "So now that I know y'all can spell start, what does that stand for?"

We all looked at each other kinda confused.

"S-T-A-R-T," he yelled. "That stands for *Stop Talking And Really Try*."

"Really try what?" David asked.

"Again, that's up to you," Harley answered. "But whatever it is, don't put it off. Do it! People sit around their whole lives talking about what they're going to do, but they never do it. Oh, but they keep saying that someday they will. That's what I meant a minute ago by people having a bad case of the somedays. They keep putting it off and putting it off, but they never start."

"Let me put it another way," he continued. "Whatever it is you've got to do, be fixing to do it, instead of doing it one of these days."

"Huh?" David asked. "What's the difference?"

"There's a big difference between fixing to and one of these days," Harley said.

"How so?" I asked.

"It's what I call southern time," Harley said.

"Is there a difference between southern time and any other time?" Will asked. "I mean, other than the time zones?"

"Oh, there sure is," Harley said. "Because in the south, there are different levels of time."

"There are?" David asked.

"I've got to hear this," Brewer said.

"Okay," Harley said. "First of all, there's fixing to. Then there's in a little bit, then there's after a while. After that comes before too long. Last is one of these days."

"Wait, there's a difference in all of those?" I asked.

Harley looked down hard at me before answering. "There sure is. Fixing to is what you're doing right this moment." Then he gave an example. "'I'm fixing to go to the snack bar, wanna come with me?'"

"In a little bit is a few minutes," he continued. "Well, I was going to the snack bar in a little bit, why don't you wait and go with me? After a while is an hour or two. 'Okay, but I've got to go to the library after a while, so hurry up.'"

We were starting to get the picture.

"Then before too long is in a day or two," Harley said. "'Speaking of the library, I need to get started on my book report before too long.' And the longest period of southern time is one of these days. That could be a few weeks, it could be several years. 'You know, one of these days I'm going to write a book myself.'"

"I never thought about that," Brewer said. "But it's true."

"It is," Harley agreed. "That's what I mean when I say you need to be fixing to do something instead of saying you'll do it one of these days. Fixing to is right this very second. One of these days is too far off. Maybe never. So be fixing to do what you need to do, instead of waiting to do it one of these days."

"So instead of talking about it, do it," Brewer said. "Is that what you mean?"

Harley got a big grin and slightly nodded toward him before saying, "Exactly, young man. Exactly. Because there's no telling how many great things were never done, just because whoever was gonna do it said they'd do it one of these days."

He then stood up off the rock. "Now that wasn't so bad, was it?" he asked. "See you next Monday."

As he started to walk away, Brewer called out, "Hey, Harley." Harley turned around and lifted his eyebrows to show that he was listening as Brewer continued. "How'd you know we were seniors?"

"How's that?" Harley asked as he cupped his hand behind his ear.

"Last week when you first asked us to meet with you, you said we were seniors," Brew said. "So if you don't mind me asking, how'd you know that?"

Harley let out one of those loud, contagious giggles, then answered as he walked on. "Boys, there's nothing that goes on at this school that I don't know."

# CHAPTER FOUR

Same hill, same rock Harley was sitting on wearing the same cap. We all sat down on the same piece of grass and looked at the same view. Same everything as last week, only a different Monday.

Then we looked down at the river while enjoying the cool breeze that felt good after practice. There was a song called *Sweet Virginia Breeze* that became popular in the beach music genre. Maybe this was that very breeze they were talking about. After a few seconds we all directed our attention to Harley.

"No, no," he insisted. "There's no hurry. I see y'all are already taking my advice from last week. Enjoying that view that you'll be missing next year. So take it in. Like I promised you, I won't take up much of your time each week. Come on, let's all enjoy that view for a few more seconds."

We did just that. Harley even took his cap off for a moment to take it all in.

"Now!" he started, slapping his knees. That got our attention and we all turned back to him.

Then he continued. "I was watching the last few minutes of your practice and I noticed something. Sometimes you're walking, sometimes you're running. How'd you learn to do that? Walk, that is?"

"I don't remember," Will said. "I was just a baby."

We all laughed, Harley did too. "That's right," he said. "You were just a baby. But even though you don't remember it, I bet you do know the answer to this. Did you walk all the way across the room on your first try?"

"I did," Will quickly said.

"That's funny," Harley responded. "A second ago you said you didn't remember."

We all gave Will a sarcastic "Oooohh" to let him know Harley had burned him. He simply looked down and nodded his head in both agreement and embarrassment.

"No, it's alright," Harley said. "None of us remember. And the answer is no. Absolutely, no. We didn't walk across the room the first time we tried. We made it probably just one step before our parents caught us. Then maybe two steps. Then three or four. Eventually you were walking so far, your mama and daddy couldn't catch you. But when you fell, the diaper's padding helped a little. You don't remember that either, but it did."

He paused for a few seconds. Maybe it was for dramatic effect. Whatever it was, it worked, because we hung on to his next word.

"Then what happened?" he asked. "Did you stop after you learned to walk?"

We all shook our heads.

"That's right," he continued. "You didn't settle for just walking, you kept going. You wanted to run."

"It gets you there faster," I said.

"Running also helps when a player for the other team is coming up behind you," David added.

Harley grinned before answering, "Yes, it does. But whatever the reason, and there are plenty of them, you wanted to run. We all do. First you walk, then you run. Most little kids run all the time. So you perfect running. Then what?"

None of us answered, so he went on. "You learn to ride a bike. I bet you probably remember that."

"Sort of," Brewer answered. "I definitely remember it more than learning to walk or run."

"Either way," Harley said. "When you first got on a bike, did you ride all the way down the block? NO! The first thing you did was learn on training wheels. Then when your daddy took off those training wheels, I'm sure he held the bike while you peddled, then he let go.

Then what happened?"

"We busted our butts," I said.

"That's right, you did," Harley said, almost excited. "You busted your butts. Sure, your daddies might have tried to catch you, but catching a kid falling off a bike is harder than catching one falling on his rear trying to walk. I bet you had plenty of skinned knees from that."

"And elbows," David said.

"Yep," Harley agreed. "And who knows what else. But did you stop? Did falling down keep you from learning to ride that bike? Nope, you kept on. Fall after fall, bloody knees and elbows aside, you kept on. And pretty soon you were riding down the block, then down the street, then all over the neighborhood. After a while you could probably all ride with no hands. You probably couldn't believe you ever thought it was hard to ride a bike because you could do it so well."

Another long pause before he continued. "And then what?"

We all sat in silence.

"Come on, then what?" he almost yelled.

"Then what, what?" Will asked. "I'm not following."

"Did you settle for riding a bike?" Harley asked. "Did you think that's how you'd get around for the rest of your lives?"

"We learned to drive," David said.

"That's right," Harley said. "You learned how to drive. But did you hop in a car and go right on the interstate? No, it took even more time. First you took drivers education. Then you got your learner's permit. Then you rode around with your parents in the car while they yelled at you because you didn't know what you were doing."

We all laughed. "My parents still yell at me when I drive them anywhere," Will said.

Harley nodded his head in agreement. "And it's a good chance they probably always will," he said. "Nobody ever gets used to seeing their baby drive a car. Now, do you see where I'm going with this?"

"Not exactly," Brewer admitted.

"Well, that's okay," Harley continued. "There's gonna be a whole lot of things that you won't see where I'm going. But just hang on, because it will all make sense. I promise."

"We trust you," I said.

"That's good," Harley went on. "Because here's my point. You didn't give up on trying to walk. You didn't give up on trying to run. You didn't give up on learning to ride a bike and then learning to drive a car. Did you?"

Again, we all shook our heads.

"As kids we don't give up," Harley explained. "We want to walk, we want to run, we want to ride a bike, we want to drive a car, and nothing or nobody is going to stop us, is it?"

"Nope," Will said, as the rest of us all nodded in agreement.

"But what happens as adults?" Harley asked. "Way too many adults give up. The same determination they had as kids to do whatever it takes seems to go away. It's kind of sad when you think about it. As kids, nothing gets in our way. But as adults, we let the littlest things stop us. Just like walking, running, riding a bike and driving a car each got harder, things we have to do as adults will get even harder."

"So why do adults stop trying?" David asked.

"Nobody knows for sure," Harley answered. "And not all adults do give up. The successful ones keep going. As a kid you had some scratches on your body learning to walk and ride a bike. Then you may have put a scratch on a car while learning to drive."

We all laughed and looked over at Brewer. "What?" he asked, as if he didn't know.

"I won't even ask," Harley said through a grin.

"Let me put it this way, Harley," I said. "Brew thinks stop signs are optional and speed limits are just suggestions."

"So you've had a few scratches then?" Harley asked Brewer. "But successful adults don't let a few scratches keep them from moving on. You can bet that every great person had some failures along the way. Many had a lot. I'll just call those failures the scratches of life. Now when you have a huge desire to do something, you might say that you're itching to do that. But when something on your body itches, you scratch it, right? And why is that?"

"Because scratching makes the itch go away," I said.

"That's right," he continued. "While it's okay to scratch something that itches, don't let the scratches of life take away what you're itching to do. You can bet that every great basketball player missed most of their shots when they first started playing. Every golfer that won The Masters completely missed the ball a whole bunch of times before they finally put on that green jacket. Every bestselling author got tons of rejection letters. Every great business person had some companies that didn't make it along the way."

We all nodded in understanding.

"I could go on and on with examples," Harley said. "But you see my point, don't you? The great ones don't give up. They keep moving on despite the setbacks and not knowing what they're doing when they first start out. Y'all need to do the same thing. Don't stop when you become adults. Keep moving on. A setback is just God's way of finding out how badly you want something."

He then stood up from the rock. "I'm done for now," he said. "Stay strong until we meet again."

We all got up from the ground and started to walk to our dorm. On the top of the hill, about fifty yards away from where we'd been meeting, was the headmaster's house. A three-story brick, colonial style one. Legend had it that parts of it were the original house that the Dowling family lived in when the campus was still their land. I'm not sure if that's true, but I do know that some of their furniture was donated along with the land and was now in the house as well as in the administration building.

As we got closer to the house, we could see the headmaster, Mr. Phillips, sitting in one of the rocking chairs on the front porch. At first he was hidden behind one of the tall, white columns that lined that porch. But he was obviously watching us the whole time we'd been walking that way.

"Hello, gentlemen," he yelled out. He always called every single student that. Maybe because he wanted us to feel like we were gentleman, that afternoon being no exception. He certainly was one. Always in a bow tie and blazer, he'd been headmaster at Dowling for several years. Before that, he was the assistant headmaster. Before that, a teacher. He was an alum, as was his father. I'd even heard that his grandfather was an alum as well. But I never did find that out for certain. I wasn't sure how old he was. His solid white hair probably made him look a little older than he actually was.

"Hi, Mr. Phillips," we hollered back.

"I see you've been chosen this year," he said.

As we got a little closer, Brewer asked, "Excuse me, sir. Chosen for what?"

He continued to rock in his chair before answering, "You'll see."

"We'll see what, Mr. Phillips?" Will begged.

"We'll see each other in the dining hall," Mr. Phillips said.

We all walked away, not having a clue what he was talking about.

# CHAPTER FIVE

Dinner on Monday through Thursday nights meant you had to wear a coat and tie. It was a hassle sometimes. Especially after having just finished practice with not much time to take a shower and put on clothes at all, much less to get dressed up.

Dinner on Monday through Thursday nights also meant you had assigned tables. Eight people at each one. Seven students and one teacher. Table assignments were then switched about once a month. It may seem weird, but it was a good way for everyone to get to know each other instead of just sitting with their usual cliques. This way the jocks got to know the drama geeks, the math nerds got to know the preppies, the seniors got to know the freshmen, and so on. Dowling was always called a very close-knit community. Perhaps this was why. There were over two hundred kids at Dowling and everybody knew everybody. And you could still sit with your cliques at the other seventeen meals they served each week.

The only other time we had to wear a coat and tie was during chapel on Sunday nights. On a daily basis we had to wear what was called classroom dress. It was a dress code that meant no jeans, shorts or athletic shoes. Shirts had to have a collar and be tucked in. You also had to wear a belt and socks.

When the weekends rolled around you could wear whatever you wanted. That is, as long as you were staying on campus. If you left the school grounds, whether to go to a mixer at a girls school, or to walk the half mile to the nearest grocery store, you had to wear classroom dress. Sometimes it was a pain to have to put on a pair of khakis and a button-down shirt just to go get a bag of potato chips. But I guess it prepared us for the real world.

We had a school uniform which consisted of a navy blazer, gray dress pants, white shirt and the Dowling school tie. We only wore that on special occasions. But when we did, I must admit we looked mighty sharp all dressed the same.

The one time I can remember that any of us wore the school uniform, without being told to do so, was during my sophomore year. It was the night before parents' weekend began so the administration wanted everything to look perfect. We were always expected to keep our dorms clean, and our rooms were inspected every morning. But before parents' weekend each year, we had to go all out.

As an incentive, the administration offered a prize to the dorm that they chose as the cleanest. That year we cleaned our dorm really well, but we decided to add an extra touch. We knew the guys in the other dorms would just be hanging out in their rooms in classroom dress when the top members of the administration came around to inspect. I don't know whose idea it was, but when the faculty got to our dorm we were all dressed in school uniform while standing at attention outside of our rooms. Whether or not that made the difference, I still don't know. But I do know that we won the contest that year. The prize? We got to skip study hall and watch a movie.

# CHAPTER SIX

When we arrived at the top of the hill the following Monday, Harley wasn't sitting on the rock as he usually did. He was standing. We were about to sit down on the ground, but he stopped us. "Don't sit down, boys," he insisted. "We're going to take a little field trip today. Follow me."

We trailed him over a little road that went to the river. Once we crossed the road, we walked across a small field that ran along the edge of a wooded area. I had seen and passed by this field hundreds of times, but never really went into it. There was no need to do so. Nothing really to see.

Harley walked into the woods and we continued to follow him. The farther we walked in, the thicker the trees seemed to be. There was a small stream that ran through the field and into those woods. I'm not sure where it ended. It was something else that we had never really paid attention to in our years there. There was also a slight path along the stream. Suddenly Harley stopped right next to what was probably the widest spot in that stream. But it was still no more than three or four feet across.

"How many of you boys have ever been back this far in these woods?" Harley asked.

David was the only one who answered. "I run back in here sometimes. I think it's part of the cross country course."

"That's right, it is," Harley said. "That's why there's a slight path through here, from all the years of running. And that's why I brought you back here. What I'm going to tell you today has to do with the cross country team." He then paused and looked around for several seconds before continuing. "Have you ever noticed anything when you were out here running, David?"

David looked puzzled. "Like what?" he asked. "Not much to notice except the trees."

"Keep looking. All of you," Harley said. We walked in small circles looking up and down, but still couldn't see anything out of the ordinary.

"I'm not seeing anything, Harley," Brewer said. "What are we missing?"

"Remember last week I told you about not giving up, no matter what?" Harley asked.

"Yes," we all said.

"Well, right here is a great example of just that. Now look down right there, on the edge of the stream," he said as he pointed to it.

We all looked down for several seconds before Brewer pointed and asked loudly, "Is that a shoe?"

It took a few more seconds before we all saw it too. Harley laughed. "Yes, boys, that's a shoe," he said. "But not just any shoe. It's a running shoe."

It was dug several inches into the mud. You could only see part of the tongue and the hole where a foot would go in.

"Believe it or not, that shoe has been down there for at least twelve years," Harley said. "Maybe even fourteen or fifteen."

"No way," Will said.

Harley stared at him before continuing. "Yep. I couldn't make up stuff like this. There are stories around this campus that NOBODY could make up!"

Will stared back in astonishment before asking, "So how'd it get there?"

"It was during a cross country meet," Harley answered. "Like I said, it was probably when y'all were barely out of diapers. I can't remember which schools Dowling was running against that day. Usually during cross country meets there are at least three or four schools competing. That part's not important. But one boy that ran for us misjudged his jump. He'd probably jumped over this stream dozens of times between meets and practices, and with no problem. But for whatever reason, that day he didn't make it. His foot landed right on the edge in the mud."

"Seriously?" I asked.

"Yep," Harley continued. "And when he took his next step, his foot came out, but the shoe stayed behind. But guess what? He just kept on running. Even though the cross country course is three point one miles long, and this spot is only about two thirds of the way to the finish line, he didn't stop. He ran the final mile or so with one shoe."

"I can't imagine running even a hundred yards with only one shoe," David said.

"Well, he did," Harley said. "Matter of fact, he finished in about fourth or fifth place that day."

"So why is the shoe still here?" I asked him.

"Well," Harley answered. "After the meet, he was coming back to get it. But when the coach heard what happened, he insisted he leave it right here."

"Why?" Brewer asked.

"For inspiration," he answered. "Even though we've had a couple of cross country coaches come and go since then, everyone tells the team each season why that shoe is there. That way, when they start to get tired before that final mile, they can see the shoe there and know not to stop. They figure if that boy who they never even met can keep going with only one shoe, then they can keep going with two."

"Wow," Brewer and David both said at the same time.

Harley looked at both of them before moving on. "That's right, wow," he said. "When I told you last week to never quit, I bet you didn't know there was a great example of a Dowling alum not quitting, and only a few hundred yards away from where you walk every single day."

"I sure didn't know it," I said.

"Me either," David added. "And I've run through here tons of times."

"Well, I've made my point for the week." Harley said. "Next Monday we'll meet back at the rock, as usual. But let me tell you, this won't be the last time we leave that rock so that I can show you something around this campus."

"Like what?" David asked.

"Oh, you'll just have to wait and see," Harley answered. "And you'll be amazed at how much has gone on at this campus in all the years it's been here. Things you haven't noticed. Or maybe you have, but you just never noticed how significant they were. And there are lots more stories to tell too."

"Can you give us a hint?" Will asked.

Harley looked back over his shoulder at us before answering. "Nope. One week at a time, boys. One week at a time."

## CHAPTER SEVEN

Fall weather was starting to kick in across the commonwealth of Virginia. The "Sweet Virginia Breeze" was turning into a slight chill. The football team was having a very mediocre season. I don't know if it was the cooler weather, or the fact that several weeks of football had us in better shape, but the walk up the hill to meet with Harley seemed a little easier.

As usual, Harley was already sitting on the rock waiting for us. We each grabbed some ground even before he had a chance to tell us to do so. Then we all looked up to see what he had to tell us that week. He took a deep breath, then one of his signature dramatic pauses before beginning. "Boys," he said. "You're lucky. Very lucky. You've all found each other here and become really good friends, haven't you?"

"I guess so," Brewer answered.

Will pointed to Brew before jokingly asking, "Wait, what was your name again?"

We all chuckled as Harley continued. "That's exactly the sort of thing I'm going to talk about now. That fact that y'all can joke around with each other and just be yourselves, and still keep hanging out together is a good thing. Not many people have that."

"They don't?" David asked.

"Not really," Harley said. "There's an old saying that if in your entire life you have just one or two truly good friends, then you've done well. Now here y'all are with each other at such a young age. And you're not just friends, you're good friends."

"That's true," I said.

"Don't most people have a lot of friends, though?" Brewer asked.

"Friends, yes. Good friends, no." Harley answered.

Brew and I both sort of asked the same question together. "Is there a difference?"

"Oh, there's a big difference," Harley insisted.

"What is it?" I asked.

Harley looked down at me, then across at all of us before answering. "Well, for starters, there are three different levels of knowing somebody. There's an acquaintance, a friend, and a good friend. And there is definitely a difference in the three."

"Well, I can't wait to hear this," Will said as he leaned forward.

Harley grinned. "Then I'll be glad to tell you. Let's say you're at the grocery store and you see somebody you know. If it's just an acquaintance, you won't even stop pushing your cart, you'll just speak to them in passing."

He stood up to act out his example, then put his hands in a fist position just above his waist as if he were pushing a cart in a store as he looked off to the side, pretending to speak to someone. "Hey, how are you? Good to see you. How's your mama doing? Bless her heart. Well, take care."

"See now, that's an acquaintance," Harley explained as he sat back down on the rock. "But let's say you see someone else at the store. If that person is a friend, you're not just gonna speak to them in passing. You'll stop your cart and talk to them for a few minutes. Maybe several, just catching up. That's a friend. But then a good friend is somebody that you'll call as soon as you can and say, 'I just saw so and so at the store and you're not gonna believe what they told me.'"

We all laughed as Brewer said, "I think I get it."

"That is true," David added.

"It is," Harley said. "That's why just a few good friends are so rare, but also so important."

He then took off his Dowling cap and rubbed his head

before looking at the view of the river. After several seconds he continued. "You know what? Y'all are probably gonna be friends for life. I'll bet you'll be in each other's weddings. Maybe even be the godfather to each other's children."

"Don't be thinking too far ahead," Will said.

"I'm not," Harley said. "But I've been here a long time and I know how things are. That's why I said you're lucky to have already found each other. You're good friends. And a good friend isn't just someone you hang out with, it's somebody who stands by you no matter what."

"But isn't that what friends do?" asked Will.

"Nope," Harley continued. "That's what GOOD friends do. That's why you should never waste your time hanging out with people who will bring you down, because that person isn't a friend. A real friend will pick you up. While other people are telling you what you can't do, a real friend will tell you what you can do."

We all sat in silence, just looking up at the man. Then he went on. "Or let me put it another way. It takes courage to do a lot of things. But just a few letters before the word courage makes all the difference in whether you do those things or not."

"What letters?" Brewer asked.

"Once again, I'm glad you asked," Harley answered.

"Those letters are D-I-S and E-N." If you put the letters D-I-S before the word courage, what does that spell?

"Discourage," we all answered together.

"Exactly," Harley said, slightly standing up. "Now, if you put the letters E and N before the word courage, what does that spell?"

Again, we all answered at the same time, "Encourage."

"Y'all are so smart," Harley said. "Encourage. And is there a difference between the words discourage and encourage?"

"Of course," Brewer answered. "One is telling you what you can't do, the other is telling you what you can do."

"You're right again," Harley said. "But what's scary is that even though those two words are completely opposite, they're only separated by a few letters. Think what a huge difference those letters can make in someone's life. You can make or break someone's decision just by whether or not you decide to put the letters D-I-S or the letters E and N in front of the word courage."

"That makes a lot of sense," David said.

"Right," Harley said, getting more excited and animated with each sentence. "And just think how many dreams have been crushed or reached, simply because of which letters someone added before courage."

"The power of the alphabet, who knew?" Will said.

"So, boys, I'll just leave you with this," Harley said as he stood up and looked down at us. "Don't hang out with people who discourage. Hang out with people who encourage. And not only should you hang out with people who will do that for you, but you should do the same for others. Don't discourage others, encourage others."

"Got it, Harley," I said.

"Good," he replied. "I'll see you next week." He started to walk away, then turned around to say one more thing. "I hear you've got a dance with one of the girls schools this weekend."

"That's right," Will said with a big grin on his face.

Harley grinned back, then made his point. "Well, have fun. But just remember, every girl is somebody's daughter and probably somebody's sister. So treat them the same way you'd want some guy to treat your sister. Understand?"

We did.

## CHAPTER EIGHT

Later that night I had trouble falling asleep. That didn't happen very often. Usually our days were so busy, I was pretty worn out by the time for lights out. Lights out was 11:00 for seniors, 10:30 for everyone else.

I was staring at the ceiling thinking about what Harley said earlier that day, about having people around you that encourage and don't discourage. I thought back to a good example of that. Something that I experienced earlier in the school year.

At Dowling, every student was required to be in a club. They could choose from among several, but they had to be in one. They met once a week between classes and athletics. They shortened each class on that day, just a little bit, to make room for club time. My freshman year I signed up for a club that was right up my alley. It was called "The Bogart/Cagney Society." We watched old movies.

The faculty advisor, and the one who started that

club, was Mr. Clifford. He was the admissions director. He didn't teach any classes or coach any sports, but somehow I got to know him really well over the years.

He was the perfect person to start up that club. To say he was a movie buff was an understatement. If you wanted to know who won the Oscar for best supporting actress in 1946, not only could he tell you, but he could also tell you the other nominees that they beat out that year. He would then give you his opinion of who should have won and who should have been nominated that got snubbed.

Though he liked and knew a lot about all kinds of movies, he was sort of a man's man and tended to prefer gangster, war and western ones. Those were the ones he showed us. There were to be no musicals or romance movies seen in that club. Looking back, some of what became my all-time favorite movies were ones I saw for the first time in that club. It was also the only club on campus where we were required to wear a coat and tie.

I loved that club and planned on being in it again for my senior year. But in the first week of school I was asked to be on the yearbook staff. It counted as a club, so I couldn't be in both. I didn't know what to do. I really wanted to stay in the movie club, but I thought being on the yearbook staff would look better on a college application, and I would be working on those soon. I only had a few days to decide.

On the morning of decision day, I was walking across campus when Mr. Clifford drove by. He stopped and rolled down his window. He knew I was having a hard time making a decision because I had spoken to him about it two days earlier.

"Have you made up your mind about what you're going to do?" he asked.

I had, but I hated to tell him. "Yes," I said, with my head hanging slightly down. "I really want to stay in the movie club, but I think being on the yearbook staff will look better on a college application."

"That's true," he said. "But you know what else would look good on a college application?"

"No, sir. What?" I asked.

"Being president of The Bogart/Cagney Society," he answered.

I lifted my head and looked at him a bit confused. "But I'm not the president," I said.

"You are now," he replied. Then he drove off without saying another word as I stood there in stunned silence for several seconds.

If that wasn't a prime example of being encouraged instead of discouraged, I don't know what was. I'm not sure if being president of that club meant anything to college admission offices or not. But what Mr. Clifford did that day would always mean a lot to me. And we saw a lot of great movies that year.

# CHAPTER NINE

As we started to walk up the hill the next Monday, we noticed that Harley wasn't there. We thought he might just be running a little late, then we heard a horn honking behind us. We looked back and saw him sitting in one of the school pickup trucks on the road that ran next to the football field. "Come on," he yelled to us. "We're taking a little trip."

As we got closer, Harley said, "One of you can ride up front with me. The rest of you can ride in the back." Somehow, Brew ended up riding shotgun. David, Will and I climbed in the back, not sure where we were heading.

We rode the short distance down to the edge of the river. Harley got out, so the rest of us did as well. He reached back into the truck cab and grabbed a small duffle bag. Something else he had with the Dowling logo on it. We walked about fifty feet from the end of the paved road to the school dock. I didn't know what he had in that bag, but I had a feeling we were about to find out.

We followed him to the end of the dock, then he stopped and took a long look at the water before he began. "Alright, boys, let's go fishing."

We all looked at each other for a second before David asked what we were all wondering. "Do you have rods?"

Harley's eyes and grin both widened before he continued. "Oh, you don't need rods to fish. Just watch this."

He put his duffle bag down on the dock, then unzipped it and pulled out a large frying pan. Without saying a word to us, he turned and walked to the edge of the dock. Then he held the frying pan out over the water and started yelling, "HERE, FISH. HERE, FISHY FISHY. COME ON. COME ON!"

Again, we all looked at each other, then looked back at him wondering if he'd gone crazy.

He looked back at us over his shoulder, then asked, "How many fish do you reckon I'll catch today?"

"Like that?" Will asked. "I'm guessing none."

Harley walked back over and put the frying pan back in the duffle bag. "Yep," he said. "You're exactly right. I won't catch any fish just holding a frying pan over the water. And no matter how loud I yell, no fish are just gonna jump in the pan, are they?"

We all shook our heads as Brewer chimed in, "I doubt it."

"That's right," Harley said. "You can't expect to catch a fish that way. You need a rod. And on the end of that rod, you need a line with a hook. And on that hook, you need some bait, don't you?"

"That makes it easier," I said.

"Right again," Harley said with his usual enthusiasm. "So why is it that in life we sometimes expect to get something without doing what we have to do to get it?"

I guess he could tell we weren't quite following him, so he went further. "You're all trying to get into colleges this year. Do you think colleges are going to send you acceptance letters, or will you have to apply first?"

"We have to apply," David answered.

"And it's a huge pain," Will said.

"I'm sure it is," Harley said. "But will it be worth it if you do your part? Of course it will. Then after you get out of college, do you think your phones will be ringing off the hook with people offering you jobs? Or will you first have to send out some resumes, then go in for interviews?"

"It'd be nice if it were that easy," I said. "But obviously you have to send out resumes first."

"Obviously is right," Harley said. "But just like with college applications, it'll pay off too. And there will be other times in life where you have to do your part. Life is full of things like that. Almost every day you'll be in situations where things don't happen if you don't do something to make them happen."

"That's true," David said.

Harley shook his head before continuing, "And here's another example. Y'all just came from football practice. You practice every day. Would you ever consider just going out and playing a game without practicing first? No! You have to practice, which is doing your part, before you can expect to win."

We all stood in silence listening to the river slap against some rocks on the bank as Harley stared at us with one of his long pauses. He took a deep breath, then continued. "And tonight, you'll probably all study for that world history test you've got tomorrow. That is, if you want to get a good grade. There are a million examples of how you need to do your part first if you expect to get anything out of life. I could go on, but you get my point. Now get back in the truck, I'll drive you to your dorm."

Somehow, Brew got to ride shotgun again. As we rode back up, Will asked David and me, "How'd he know we have a world history test tomorrow?"

"Don't you remember," I said. "There's nothing that goes on at this school that he doesn't know."

## CHAPTER TEN

The next Monday Harley was waiting for us on the hill. We had barely sat down before he began.

"Now, boys," he said. "Last week we went down to the dock. But I'm betting that wasn't your first time down there, was it?"

"Not even close," Brewer confirmed.

"That's what I thought," Harley said. "So let me ask you this. In all the times you've been down there, have you ever been crabbing?"

"Yep," Will answered. "And not just once."

"Good," Harley continued. "I figured so. And when you went crabbing, did you catch anything?"

"Usually," Brewer said.

Harley rubbed his chin as he looked over at Brew,

then asked, "How many?"

"That depends," Brewer said. "Sometimes several, sometimes just one or two."

"Okay," Harley continued. "And when you caught them, what did you put them in?"

"A bucket," Brewer answered.

"Good. That's usually the best way to do it," Harley said. "I find that if you try to hold on to them, it can pinch a little bit."

We all laughed as I said, "I hate when that happens."

"We all do," Harley agreed. "Now, when you have a bucket full of crabs, have you ever looked into that bucket to see what they're doing?"

"They're usually not very happy," David said.

"Actually, I guess they're pretty crabby," Will said. "Get it? Crabby?"

We all groaned. Harley just rolled his eyes before moving on. "Yeah, they're not very happy in that bucket. But what are they trying to do in there?"

"Get out?" I asked.

"Exactly," Harley said. "They're trying to get out.

But why don't they?"

"Usually another crab is pulling them back down," David said.

Harley pointed to David and practically shouted. "Say that again!"

Not certain if he'd said something wrong, David hesitated before repeating himself. "Usually another crab is pulling them back down."

I guess Harley could sense his hesitation. "Don't be nervous," he said. "Because you're exactly right."

David smiled as if he'd just found out he got a perfect score on his SAT.

Harley continued. "Why do you reckon crabs pull other crabs down?"

Again, David wasn't certain, but he answered anyway. "Because they don't want them to get to the top of the bucket."

Will laughed at him, then asked. "Why would a crab care if another crab gets to the top of a bucket?"

Before David could respond, Harley jumped in. "Actually, he's right. They are trying to stop the other crabs from getting to the top."

"Why?" Will asked

"Good question," Harley said. "Why would a crab care if another crab got to the top? Anyone care to take a guess?"

"Because they figure if they're at the bottom of the bucket, the other crabs need to be too," Brew said. "Or am I way off?"

"Nope," Harley said as he smiled at Brew. "Actually, you're right on. As crazy as it may seem, crabs don't seem to want other crabs to climb to the top of the bucket. And you know what? Sometimes in life, people are the same way."

"You mean people are crabby?" Will asked.

"You're just full of crab jokes today, aren't you?" I asked.

"Well, some people are sure crabby in life," Harley said. "But what I mean is, just like crabs pull each other down from the top, some people will try to pull you down when you're trying to climb to the top. Not to the top of a bucket, but to the top of life."

"Or maybe the top of the ladder," Brewer said.

"Whatever that ladder may be," I added.

"Exactly," Harley said. "Boys, y'all are hot today. And you're right. Whatever that ladder may be. Because everybody has a different ladder in life. But no matter what your ladder may be, you've got to climb it. But sure enough, some people are going to try to pull you down."

"Why?" David asked.

"Again, that's a good question," Harley answered. "Maybe just like those crabs, they don't want you to climb high while they're still at the bottom. They figure if they're down, you should be too. But here's the beauty. Crabs probably can't stop other crabs from pulling them down. But you can stop other people from pulling you down."

"We can?" David asked

"Absolutely," Harley insisted. "Remember recently when I said that you have to have courage, but that some people will try to encourage you while others try to discourage you?"

"Yes," we all said nodding our heads.

"That's why I said you have to hang around people who will encourage you and not discourage you," Harley continued. "In life, some people are going to try to pull you down. But others are going to help you up."

Then Harley stood up and bent slightly over. He put his hands together palms up and locked his fingers making a small step. "That's why you should always hang out with people who will not only help you to the top, they'll join their two hands together like this to give you a boost," he said.

Then he took his cap off and looked down at us.

"And just remember," he concluded. "Crabs don't have any choice of who they share their bucket with. If they're being pulled down, it's not their fault. But you do have a choice as to who you share your time with. So make sure you spend it with people who won't pull you down. Otherwise, you'll stay in a bucket. And nobody wants that."

He put his cap back on, then turned to walk away before saying, "Come on, boys, it's almost dinner time."

## CHAPTER ELEVEN

Usually Harley was already sitting on the rock before we got to our meeting place. But this week he was standing. He waited until we'd all been seated on the ground, then he sat down on the rock.

"Boys," he began with a big grin. "Do you want to hear a joke?"

"Yeah. Let's hear it," we all said.

"Of course you do," Harley said. "Who doesn't want to hear a joke? Have you ever asked someone if they want to hear a joke, then had them say that they didn't?"

"Why would somebody not want to hear a joke?" Will asked.

"Why is right," Harley answered. "Everybody wants to hear a joke. Even if you're in a hurry, you'll stop to hear a joke. Now why do you suppose that is?"

"Because everybody likes a good joke," Brewer said.

"That's right," Harley agreed. "But why do they like a good joke?"

We all looked at each other a little confused before Will said, "Because they're funny."

"You're getting warmer," Harley said.

We continued to look around in silence before Harley continued. "What do people do when they hear a funny joke?"

"They laugh," I said.

"Exactly," Harley said. "They laugh. Now, do people like to laugh?"

"Of course," I said.

"That's right," Harley said. "Everybody likes to laugh, and everybody likes to hear laughter. Let me ask you this. Has there ever been a time when you were sitting in your dorm room and you heard people in the next room, or out in the hall, laughing really hard?"

"It happens all the time," David said.

"Every day," Brewer jumped in. "Sometimes several times a day."

"That's good," Harley said. "And when you hear that laughter, what do you do?"

"Go see what's so funny," Will answered.

"Right again," Harley said. "You go out to see what's so funny. And why? Because when people are laughing, they're happy. So when people are happy, you want to be a part of it. Now, on the other hand, do you ever hear people arguing in your dorm?"

"Sometimes," Brewer said. "But luckily not as much as people laughing."

"Well, that's good," Harley said. "And when you do hear people arguing, what do you do?"

"Ignore it," David said.

"Sit there and wish they'd stop," I added.

"Turn up my music," Brewer said.

Harley gave a sarcastic look before asking, "You mean you don't go out and see what's going on like you do when someone is laughing?"

"Hardly," Will said. "If I do get up it's to close my door."

"And why is that?" Harley asked.

"Because I don't want to hear people arguing," Will answered.

"So let me ask again, why is that?" Harley said.

"Are you asking why I don't want to hear people arguing?" Will wondered.

"I believe I am," Harley answered.

Will shrugged his shoulders slightly before saying, "Because it's no fun being around people arguing."

"That's right," Harley said. "It's no fun being around people who are arguing. So can we all agree that it's fun to be around people who are laughing, but not around people who are arguing?"

"Right," David said.

"Now here's my point," Harley continued. "If everybody likes to laugh, then why do we do it less and less as we get older?"

"I didn't know we did," Brew said.

"Well, unfortunately, it's true." Harley said. "Matter of fact, I've read that children laugh over four hundred times a day and adults laugh only four times a day."

"Seriously?" David asked.

"I only wish I was making that up," Harley said. "Now, y'all are at an age where you still laugh a lot, but maybe not as much as you did ten years ago. And if you don't watch it, ten years from now you'll be laughing a whole lot less. Maybe not much at all."

"That's scary," I said. "Why is that?"

"I'm not really sure," Harley answered. "I just know it's a shame. I think people assume that getting older means you need to be serious. And that's hardly the case. Some people think that you can't be an adult and have fun."

"But aren't you supposed to get more mature when you get older?" David asked."

"More mature?" Harley said. "Yes. But a stick in the mud? No. Just because you're mature doesn't mean you have to be overly serious. Life's too short to have a long face."

"Did you make that up?" I asked.

"As far as I know," Harley answered.

"Can I use it?" Will asked.

"Yes, you can use it," Harley answered. "And I hope you make it your life's motto. I've got another one. You ready?"

"Yes," Brew said.

Harley stood slightly up so we knew we were in for something good. Then he said, "Acting your age is childish."

We all laughed.

He held up his hand to continue. "Now don't get me wrong. I'm not saying you should go through life acting a fool. I'm just saying don't think that just because you're old, that you have to be an old fuddy duddy."

"I've got you," Will said.

"And let me add this," Harley said. "When you get out in the real world in a few years, don't go to work thinking you can joke around all day. Do your job and do it well, just keep a sense of humor while you're doing it."

He stood up all the way which meant he was closing. "A few years back I had an alum tell me about his new boss. He would walk around the office all day, and if he saw an employee smiling, he'd give them more work to do. He thought that if an employee was smiling, they were happy. And if they were happy, they weren't busy enough. Needless to say, that alum didn't stick around there very long. Who wants to work for somebody like that?"

"Not me," David said. "Like you said, life's too short."

Harley nodded in agreement, then went on. "And I hope that when you get older, and you're the boss, you won't have the attitude that he had. You'll keep your employees around a lot longer if they're happy. Now I'll leave you with this. Laugh more in life, boys. God put all kinds of creatures on this earth, but humans are the only ones that he gave the ability to laugh. But we don't use that gift nearly enough."

He started to walk away before Will called out to

him. "You never did tell us the joke."

"Come again," Harley said.

Will continued. "When we got here today you asked us if we wanted to hear a joke. But you never told us one."

"Ok," Harley said. "Knock. Knock."

"Who's there?" we asked.

Behind a sly grin Harley said, "You'll have to come back next week to find out."

# CHAPTER TWELVE

Harley was standing up when we arrived at the top of the hill the next Monday. I had a feeling that meant we were in for a little field trip. Sure enough, he waved his arm and said, "Follow me."

We didn't ask any questions, we just followed him. Almost in a single file line like baby ducks following their mother, we walked across campus trying to figure out where we were going. As we approached each building and place, I would wonder if that was where we were going to stop. The possible location of our next lesson decreased with each step. Finally, we stopped in front of school library.

Harley turned and looked back at us before beginning. "Do y'all know what this place is?" he asked, pointing to the door.

"Is this another trick question?" Will asked.

"I hope not," Harley answered. "It should be pretty

obvious."

"It's the library," David said.

"Of course it is," Harley replied. "Now what do you say we go in?"

He walked up the stairs then held the door open and stood back to let us walk in. Then he took his cap off and followed us. We all stood in the entrance waiting to see what he was up to. He walked past us, and we kept up. He went inside the main room, then stopped and looked around with his hands on his hips.

The building was pretty empty as it usually was that time of day, and almost eerily quiet. Everyone else was coming from their respective sports practice and getting ready for dinner. But between dinner and lights out it would be packed.

"What do y'all think?" Harley asked in a loud whisper.

None of us spoke, probably because we weren't sure how to answer. Then Harley helped us out a little. "It's pretty impressive, huh?" he asked.

"I guess so," Brew said.

"There's no need to guess," Harley said. "It's definitely impressive. Now look around, what do you see?"

He lifted his head up and turned in a full circle

looking up at the countless shelves. We did the same.

"So what do you see?" he asked again.

"Books," we all said together.

"That's right," Harley said. "Books. And do you realize how lucky you are?"

"About what?" Will asked.

"To have all these books," Harley answered.

"I've never thought about it," Will replied.

"Well, you should," Harley said. "Because let me say it again, but not in the form of a question…..you are all extremely lucky."

"To have books?" I asked, slightly smirking.

Harley wasn't smirking when he answered. "Yes, to have books. I'm sure y'all take it for granted, but you shouldn't. Believe it or not, this one building on this one campus has more books than many entire countries do."

"What? Why?" David asked.

Harley squinted almost in frustration as he answered. "Because sadly enough, there are some countries in this world that are run by people crazy enough to not let their citizens have books."

"I never knew that," Brew said.

"That's okay," Harley said. "Most people don't know that. But that's why you shouldn't take it for granted. Now how many times in your years at Dowling has a teacher assigned a book for you to read?"

"Way too many," Will said.

We all laughed as quietly as possible, except Harley. He just shook his head in a disgusted manner, then spoke "And I bet you hate being assigned a book to read, don't y'all?"

We were all embarrassed and hesitated before Brew said, "It's probably not our favorite thing."

"Well, maybe it should be," Harley said. "There are millions and millions of kids in this world who would love to be given a book to read. And here in America, you act like it's a chore to have to read, don't you?"

We all looked around ashamed before he continued. "I don't mean to give you a hard time. But maybe instead of thinking what a pain it is to HAVE to read a book, you should realize how lucky are to GET to read a book."

"Probably so," David said.

"I'm glad you agree," Harley responded. "Now walk with me."

We followed him until he stopped between two aisles

of rows and rows of tall shelves filled with thousands of titles.

Harley pointed to a section of books, then continued in his loud whisper. "Over there is history. Want to learn about anything that ever happened in this world? It's there." He then pointed in another direction. "Over there are the biographies. Want to learn about anybody who's ever walked on this planet? It's there." Then he pointed in another direction. "Over there is science. Want to learn how and why stuff happens? It's there." Pointing to yet another area he said, "Over there is geography. Want to know where any place is and anything about it? It's there." Pointing again he said, "And over there are all kinds of fiction books, in every genre you can think of. I could go on and on and on, but I think you're getting my point."

"I think so," I said.

"It's just this," Harley added. "There is nothing in this world that you can't find out in this building. Nothing!"

We all stood in silence, somewhat amazed.

"I'll tell you a sad statistic," Harley went on. "Only about one in a hundred Americans reads an entire book in a year. ONE IN A HUNDRED! One percent. How sad is that?"

"Pretty sad," David said.

"You're absolutely right it is," Harley agreed. "And

while most people in America aren't lucky enough to live on a campus where there's a library within walking distance, there is nobody in America that lives far from a public library. Yet most don't take advantage of that. So from now on are you boys going to take advantage of it?"

We all nodded our heads in unison.

"Okay," Harley continued. "Before I send you on your way let me ask you this. When you want to find out something, what do you do?"

"Ask someone," I said.

"That's exactly right, boy" Harley said. "If you want to find something out, you ask someone. Now, how do you spell ask?"

David was the first one to respond with the obvious answer. "A-S-K."

"That's right," Harley said. "And do you know what that means?"

"I'm guessing you're about to tell us," Will said.

Harley grinned. "And you'd be right. A-S-K stands for *Assume Someone Knows*."

"Assume someone knows what, exactly?" Brew asked.

"Anything," Harley answered. "What time it is, how

to get somewhere, what's the capital of a certain country, or who the ninth president of the United States was. There is nothing that you need to know that someone doesn't have the answer to, and all you need to do to find out that answer is to ask them. As long as you don't ask, you'll never know. Even in the Bible, the Book of Matthew says, 'Ask and ye shall find.' So do it. Because if you don't ask, you'll never know anything."

He turned and walked back towards the door which let the rest of us know that was it for this week. As he held the door open for us again he said, "Hold on, y'all."

We all stopped outside on the top of the library steps to see what he was going to tell us. Then he joined us, and as he put his cap back on he said, "It was William Henry Harrison."

"What?" Will asked.

"The ninth president of the United States. It was William Henry Harrison," he continued. "And he served the shortest term of any other president. He died after only about a month in office."

"How on earth do you know that?" I asked.

Harley grinned and pointed back to the library before trotting down the steps and answering, "I read it in there."

## CHAPTER THIRTEEN

The days were getting shorter and the fall sports season was coming to a close. We were entering our final week of football practice with one game to go in a few days. We were .500 at that point. If we won that last game we'd end up with a winning record. If we lost, a losing record.

Harley was already sitting on the rock when we arrived. As usual, he told us to, "Grab some ground." Which we did.

"Boys," he began. "The weather is starting to get a little colder. Pretty soon we'll be seeing birds heading south for the winter. Now how do y'all reckon those birds will get south?"

"They'll fly," David said.

"That's right," Harley responded. "They will fly. And why do you suppose they do that?"

"You mean, why do they fly?" I asked.

"Yes," Harley answered. "Why do they fly?"

"Probably because it's too far to walk," Will said.

"Well, you're getting warm," Harley responded. "But be more specific. Why do they fly?"

We all looked around at each other, not really certain what he was asking for. Finally, Brewer shouted out with, "Because they can."

Harley got really excited, then looked at Brew and asked, "Because they can what?"

"Fly?" Brew asked.

"Exactly!" Harley almost yelled. "They fly because they can. And why on earth would they walk when they have the ability to fly?"

"Of course," Brew said.

"You say, 'of course.' But does everybody always use the abilities they are given?" Harley asked.

"Probably not," Will said.

"Probably not doesn't begin to touch it," Harley replied. "We are all put on this earth with abilities, or gifts, but we don't always use them."

"We don't?" I asked.

"No, you don't. Few people do," Harley answered. "Every person ever put on this earth is given a special gift. The problem is, very few people use that special gift."

"How come?" David asked.

"Actually," Harley said, "that's a good question." Then he gave one of his dramatic pauses before continuing. "But people have enormous gifts that they just let go to waste. Let me ask y'all this. On Christmas morning, do you open gifts?"

"Oh, yeah," Will answered.

"Of course you do," Harley continued. "And do you put those gifts in the back of a closet and never use them, or do you use them right away?"

"I pretty much use mine right away," Brew answered.

"That's right, you do," Harley said. "And you should. If it's a game, you play it right away. If it's clothes, you wear them right away, and so on."

"Why shouldn't we?" I asked.

"Why shouldn't you?" Harley answered. "You were given that gift, why not use it?"

"Exactly," I said.

"But here's the thing," Harley continued. "On

Christmas morning, and on your birthdays, you'll use the gifts you're given from your family. But we all get a gift from God that we don't always use."

"We don't?" David asked.

"Nope, usually not," Harley answered. "The problem is, even though most people may know what their gift is, they are afraid to use it. Some people might ignore their gift and try to do something else that they don't really have a gift for, then wonder why they're unhappy doing that."

"I'm not really following you, Harley," I admitted.

"Well, let me put it this way," he replied. "I have a terrible singing voice. I mean just awful. There's no way you're going to ever hear me singing on a stage anywhere. But I am good at fixing things. I knew that as a kid. My favorite things to play with weren't toys, they were tools. When I was only two years old I could already tell you the difference between a doodad and a thingamajig. That's what my gift is. I love fixing things so much, I'd probably be the maintenance man here for free. Just don't tell Mr. Phillips I said that."

We all laughed as Brew said, "We won't."

"You know the old saying, if it ain't broke, don't fix it?" Harley asked.

We all nodded that we did.

Harley continued. "Well, my philosophy is, if it ain't

broke, break it so I can fix it. That's how much I love fixing things. And that's why I do what I do. But I'm not the only one at this school doing that. Every teacher, coach, cook, and so on are using their gifts and doing what they were put on this earth to do."

"I'm starting to understand," I said.

"Good," Harley replied. "Because it's not exactly hard to understand. Just use your God given gifts. Plain and simple. I'll put it another way. How do you spell the word gift?"

We all looked around to see who wanted to answer. Finally, David did. "G-I-F-T," he said.

"I have a feeling we're in for another acronym," Will said.

"And you'd be right," Harley replied. "G-I-F-T stands for *God Is Furnishing Talent*."

"I like that one," Brew said.

"Thank you," Harley responded with a smile. "I'm pretty proud of it too. And it's true. God has furnished each one of us with a talent. He didn't waste His time putting us here without a specific purpose. He's too busy for that."

"But you said most people don't use their gift," Brewer said.

"And they don't," Harley went on. "That's what is

sad. But that's why I'm here today to encourage each of you to find your gift and use it."

"How do we do that?" I asked.

"Again, it's not hard." Harley answered. "And most people probably overthink it. But all you have to do is realize what you love doing. What you think about all the time. What you know you're really good at. That's your gift. You see, God doesn't just give us a gift. He also gives a burning desire to use it. Whatever you enjoy doing. Whatever you know you're really good at doing. That's what He wants you to be doing."

"Gotcha," Brew said.

"But let me take it another step further," Harley said. "You're all on teams each season. Do you play different positions or the same one?"

"Different ones," David said.

"Exactly," Harley said. "And why is that?"

"Because we'd be pretty bad if we all played the same position," Will said.

We all laughed but Harley held up his hand to stop us. "Don't laugh," he said. "Because he's right. Imagine how bad teams would be if everybody played the same position. The quarterback wouldn't have anybody to throw to. The pitcher wouldn't have anybody to catch. And it's not just sports. Imagine if you went to a concert and everybody played the same instrument. It'd be pretty hard to listen to. But when everybody plays a different instrument, it all comes together, doesn't it?"

We all nodded again.

Harley continued. "When you get older, the places where you'll work will have different departments with people using their different talents. Just like I said everybody working here found their gift. But they got more specific. They don't just teach, they teach exactly what subject they enjoy. And in the office some people work in admissions, some people in development, some in the accounting department, and so on. I could go on with a bunch of examples, but you get the point. If we all use our God given talent, then we'll all be happy. And like I said a couple of weeks ago, life's too short to be taken seriously."

"I remember that one," I said.

"Good," he responded. "And let me add one more thing. You all agreed that on Christmas morning you don't wait to use your gifts, right?"

"Right," Will answered.

"So remember this," Harley said. "Don't wait to use the gift you were born with. Another word for gift is present. And there's no better time to use your gift than the present."

"Wow," David said.

"Okay," Harley said. "Next Monday you won't be

coming from the football field, you'll be coming from basketball practice."

"Why am I not surprised that you knew we're all on the basketball team?" Brewer said.

"Of course I know," he said. "So because of that, and the weather getting colder, let's do this. Meet me after basketball practice on the top row of the bleachers. How does that sound?"

"Can't get any easier than that," Will said.

"Good. I'll see you next Monday," Harley said as he stood up from the rock.

"Hey, Harley," Brew said.

Harley turned around and looked at him.

"Two weeks ago you started a joke and said you'd finish it the next week," Brewer said. "Well, next week was last week and you didn't finish it."

"You're right," Harley said. "So here goes. Knock knock."

"Who's there?" we all asked.

"Orange," Harley answered.

"Orange who?" we said.

"Orange you glad you agreed to meet with me every

week this year?" He laughed hard, turned back around and walked away.

## CHAPTER FOURTEEN

Fall sports were officially over. We did manage to win our last football game of the season, giving us a winning record. Barely. Now it was time to move on to winter sports and my favorite sport of all – basketball. Not just to play, but to watch as well.

All four of us played basketball, but Brewer and I didn't start. Brew, at least, was usually the first guy off the bench. I was always the last guy in, and that was if I got in the game at all. Will and David were both in the starting lineup. David was really good.

The gym was named for a headmaster who had been there for almost thirty years but had retired long before I arrived at Dowling. After the first practice on Monday, Harley was sitting on the top row of the bleachers as promised. I wasn't sure how long he'd been there and how much of our practice he'd seen.

We walked to the top and sat on the row of bleachers under him. He was holding his cap in his hand. He was inside, after all.

He took a long pause, then began. "Boys," he said. "There's no telling how many games I've seen in this gym. Between both the varsity and junior varsity games, probably hundreds. I've seen some really close games, and I've seen some real blowouts too."

"I don't doubt that," Brewer said.

"Yep," he continued. "There have been several times that I've seen games won on a last second shot that went in and lost on a last second shot that rimmed out. It's amazing how less than an inch of where the ball goes can end up deciding who wins…..and who loses."

"That's why I love this game," I said.

"Me too," Harley agreed. "And in many ways, life is much the same. Sometimes the smallest things can make the difference between winning and losing. You have to do your best to control which way the ball goes. But sometimes, no matter how hard you try, the ball just isn't going to bounce the way you want it to. You just have to make the best of the outcome and move on."

We all nodded our heads in agreement.

"Now," Harley said. "I want to tell you a story of my favorite memory of any game I have ever seen here. It was about ten years ago. Dowling had made it to the state playoffs and we had homecourt advantage for the first round. There was a boy on the team who was in the starting lineup, but he was hardly the best guy on our team. Put it this way, he was just barely in the starting lineup."

"I can relate to that," Will laughed.

"He wasn't a bad player," Harley went on. "I guess he was good for a few points and rebounds a game, but that was about it. Now in this particular game it was late in the second quarter. The game was tied with just a few seconds left before halftime. There was a loose ball at midcourt and several players dove for it. The ball popped out and this kid picked it up, dribbled down to the basket and made a layup just as the buzzer sounded. His first bucket of the game."

"Cool," I said.

"That's what he thought too," Harley replied. "After the ball went in, he turned around with a big smile on his face. Only he realized quickly that none of his teammates were smiling. And instead of the home crowd cheering, there was dead silence."

"Why?" David asked.

"You won't believe it," Harley answered. "When he picked up the loose ball, he got so excited that he didn't realize he was dribbling the wrong way. He scored a basket for the other team."

"You're kidding," Will said.

"I wish I was," Harley said. "So instead of us leading by two at the halftime, we were losing by two."

"Man, I feel bad for him," David said.

"Oh, you should have seen the look on his face when he realized what had happened," Harley said. "He went from a big smile to a look of horror and just stood there, under the basket, for several seconds."

"That would stink," Brewer said.

"At the time it did," Harley agreed. "And he was the last guy to walk off the court. With his head hung low too."

"I bet," I said.

"He probably thought he was going to get yelled at in the locker room," Harley continued. "But instead, the coach didn't even mention it. He gave them their instructions for the second half, then said, 'The same guys who started the game will start the second half.'"

"Seriously?" Brew asked. "The coach kept him in the game?"

"He did," Harley answered. "And that kid was as surprised as anybody. He even looked at the coach and said, 'I'm still in the game?' The coach said, 'Of course you are.' Then the boy said, 'But I messed up. I put the ball in the wrong basket.' The coach smiled and said, 'You did put the ball in the other basket, but you know that in the second half the teams switch baskets. So I don't think you messed up, you were just planning ahead for the second half.'"

"That's awesome," I said.

"It is," Harley agreed. "And it must have done something for his confidence. Because in the second half he scored eleven points. Normally he was lucky if he scored that many in two whole games. And, of course, we won that game. Without his eleven points, we may not have."

"What a good story," David said.

Harley nodded his head in agreement. "And a good lesson too. Imagine if the coach had benched him. What would that have done for his confidence? He would have never lived that moment down. But instead, the coach gave him the opportunity to redeem himself. And that he did."

"It sure sounds that way," Brew said.

Harley went on. "That's why in life we have to surround ourselves with people who will believe in us. And we have to believe in others. As I said a while back, when you get out in the real world, work for people who believe in you. Then when you become the boss, believe in others that work for you."

"Like you told us, don't discourage, encourage," I said.

"I'm glad you've listened and remembered what I've told you," Harley said as he stood up. "Until next week, boys."

## CHAPTER FIFTEEN

Later that night I was in bed having trouble falling asleep again. I was thinking about what Harley had said about the kid who put the ball in the wrong basket. His coach believed in him and it paid off. He was right that sometimes when a person stands behind you, it makes all the difference in the world.

While I said that Brew, Will, David and I were on the basketball team, that was true. Only this was the first year that I actually played on the team. The previous three years I was the statistician. Or the official bookkeeper as it was called. I would sit at the scorer's table between the two benches, along with a representative from the other school that we were playing, as well as the person who ran the clock. When a foul was called, the refs told us who it was on. It was up to us to let them know if a player had fouled out, or if a team had enough fouls for the other to be shooting free throws.

The basketball coach for the varsity team was Mr.

Samuels. But everybody called him "Coach Samuels." Even when he taught a class, or even if you weren't on a team that he coached, that was what you called him.

In movies and TV shows, boarding school teachers are always portrayed as very old and very serious. Usually wearing tweed jackets with patches on the elbows, and probably holding a pipe in their mouth as they said things like, "Young man, wipe that smile off your face." But, in reality, most boarding school teachers were somewhat young and the majority of them were what we considered to be pretty cool. Coach Samuels was no exception. He was probably only a few years out of school. With his lanky frame, no one was surprised that he had played basketball in college.

I had been the official bookkeeper for the junior varsity team in my first two years, while the other three guys played. In my junior year, when they each moved up to play for the varsity team, Coach Samuels asked me to move up as the official bookkeeper. I liked doing it and he liked having me do it. But a few weeks before practice started that year I had a change of heart. I wanted to actually play on the team. I went to Coach Samuels and asked him if I could.

"Well, I'll be honest," he said. "You wouldn't get much playing time. I mean, you'd only get in late in the game when we had a huge lead. So you'd be much more valuable to me as the official bookkeeper."

"Ok," I said. I understood but was still disappointed.

A few days later I asked him again. This time he was

a little quicker with his answer. "Sorry, I can't do it."

Either too determined or maybe just too stubborn, I asked him again the next week as we passed each other on campus. Even quicker with his answer he almost yelled, "No!"

As he continued to walk in the other direction, I hollered back, "Give me one reason why I can't be on the team."

Referring to the fact that I am somewhat vertically challenged, he hollered back, "I'll give you five feet and five inches worth of reasons." Then he let out a loud laugh as if he was really proud of that one. Even Will couldn't have come up with such a great sarcastic comeback. I just stood there in silence as he walked away.

I had given up asking him and was sharpening my pencils for another season of bookkeeping. But about ten days before practice was to begin, he came up to me at lunch, put his hand on my shoulder and said, "Okay. But like I said, don't expect much playing time."

I didn't.

## CHAPTER SIXTEEN

Harley was walking up the bleachers just as our practice ended for the day. When we were meeting outside he always told us to, "Grab some ground." I guess now we were grabbing some aluminum. At least I think that's what bleachers are made of.

"Boys," he began, as he did so often. "Have you ever been discussing a movie with some people and one of them said, 'Well, it was good, but the book was better'?"

"Yes," Brew said.

"All the time," I added.

"Right," Harley agreed. "Now have you ever heard somebody say that the movie was better than the book?"

"I've haven't thought about it, but I never have heard anyone say that," Brew answered.

"Me either," David said.

"And why do you suppose that is?" Harley asked.

"I don't know," Will answered. "Because the book is always better."

"Well, maybe," Harley said. "Or maybe not. But people always THINK the book is better. And do you know why?"

We all shook our heads as I said, "Not really."

"Well, I'll tell you," Harley replied. "The reason the book is better than the movie is because when you read a book, you're the director. You're the one picturing what the characters look like and what the scenery might be. Then when you go to the movie you say, 'Well, that's not who I would have cast as the main character.'"

"That's true," David said.

"Something else I've never thought about," Brew agreed.

"But it is true," Harley said. "You control the book but not the movie. That's why you usually enjoy the book more. And let me tell you, boys, life is much the same."

"Life is like a book?" Will asked.

"When you're comparing it to a movie it is," Harley

answered. "Because just how you control a book, you can also control your life. You're the director of your life. You get to decide where you are, what you're doing and who you cast to hang out with. But if you let other people direct your life, then it doesn't turn out like you expected it to. Make sense?"

"You have a good way of explaining things," I said.

"Thank you," he said with a smile. "I said earlier that fixing things is my gift. Maybe putting things in perspective is my gift too."

"It seems to be," David said.

"Thanks again," Harley said. "Now come on, I'll walk y'all out."

We all walked down the bleachers to the gym lobby and out through the giant glass doors. Once outside, he headed one way and we headed another. All of a sudden, we heard a noise overhead. Before we had a chance to see what it was, Harley yelled out, "See that?"

We turned to look at him and saw that he was pointing up to the sky. We looked up in that direction and spotted what we'd heard. A flock of about thirty birds squawking as they went over us. We watched them for several seconds, then we looked back at Harley. He had a huge smile on his face.

"Those birds are heading south for the winter," he said. "And notice that they're all using their gift from God."

"What do you mean?" I asked.

"Look closely," he answered. "None of them are walking."

# CHAPTER SEVENTEEN

Harley was waiting for us when we got to the top of the bleachers. "Do you remember at our first meeting when I said that I'm always on time?" he asked.

"Yes," we all answered together.

"That's something my dad taught me and that his dad taught him. Always be on time. Even if you know the person you're meeting might be late, it's better to wait for someone instead of having them wait for you. If you're late, it's like you're saying that your time is more valuable than the people you're meeting. And that's not a good thing."

We all nodded in agreement.

"Now," he continued. "Who has ever read their horoscope?"

Again, we all nodded our heads. Brewer, always the

polite one, even slightly raised his hand in agreement.

"I'll admit I have too," Harley said. "Even though none of us should because it's a bunch of nonsense. But a while back I was reading it on my birthday. At the bottom of the so-called predictions they tell you what you're like if that day is your birthday. So just out of curiosity I read it. I don't remember exactly what it said, but it was all good things. It boosted my ego, you might say."

"I've read that on my birthday," Brew said. "And you're right, it only said good things."

"Exactly," Harley agreed. "A few weeks later it was my brother's birthday. Just out of curiosity I read it to see what it would say about him. Well, guess what? It said almost the exact same thing it had said about me. Almost word for word. And believe me, my brother and I are nothing alike. So for the next several days I read that part of the horoscope to see what it might say. And almost every day it was basically the same thing. It said only good, positive things about whoever might be celebrating a birthday that day. Never anything bad."

"Why do they do that?" Brew asked.

"I have a theory," Harley answered. "Deep down we all think we are full of good, positive qualities. And whoever writes those horoscopes knows that. They also know that most people aren't going to read that part every day, only on their birthday. That's why they can repeat the same positive things over and over. Because people believe that about themselves."

"Yep," I said.

"But here's the problem," Harley continued. "Even though people believe they have those good qualities, they don't always use them. Like I've said, everybody has a gift, but they don't usually use it. A stupid horoscope can tell you what you want to hear, but most people still don't take advantage of what they know they have. It's the same with what I said about the book being better than the movie. Everybody knows that, but they don't realize it's because they have control."

"True," I said again.

"It is," he agreed. "Everybody wants success, but most people don't realize they already have what it takes to get it. It's up to them. Remember in *The Wizard of Oz* when The Good Witch told Dorothy that she'd always had the power to go back to Kansas, but she had to learn it herself?"

"Yes," we all said.

"Well, that's my point," Harley said. "We all have that power, we just have to use it. Now I talked about success. How do you spell that?"

"Acronym time," Will said.

"You're right," Harley smirked. "So you spell it."

"S-U-C-C-E-S-S," Will replied.

"Perfect," Harley said. "And what's that stand for?"

"I have a feeling you're about to tell us," Brew said.

"And you'd be right," Harley agreed. "And here goes. Success stands for *Something You Can Control Every Single Second.* Got it?"

"These get better each time," I said.

"Glad you like them," Harley said. "Because I've got even more as the year goes on. Something you can control every single second. What exactly do you think that means?"

"That we're the ones who control our success," Brew said.

"Pretty much," Harley replied. "In this case, the letter U is important. It means you. Because you control your success. Not your boss. Not your friends. Not your family. YOU! You're the one. You're the director of your life. Not anybody else."

"I guess everybody kind of wants to be a movie director," Brew said.

"That's right," Harley said. "And this way, everybody can be. It's probably not easy to direct a movie, but it is easy to direct your own life. It's your life, so don't let anybody else call the shots. See you next week."

## CHAPTER EIGHTEEN

We were barely seated on our bleacher row before Harley began. "Sometimes people make excuses as to why they can't be successful," he said. "They think it's something you're either born into or you're not. But your family has nothing to do with your success, no matter what people might say. Now, how many parents do you each have?"

We all looked at one other, not sure if what seemed like such a simple question was too just that. Finally, David spoke up. "Two."

"Of course," Harley said. "So how many grandparents does that mean you have?"

"Four," I answered.

"Good," Harley said. "And how many great-grandparents?"

"Eight," I answered again.

"I didn't know any of my great-grandparents," Will added.

"That's okay," Harley insisted. "Most of us don't. Or if we do, we probably only have a vague memory of them. Now go back another generation. How many great-great-grandparents do each of you have?"

"I guess sixteen," Brewer said.

"Sixteen is right," Harley said. "Are you seeing a pattern here? The number of ancestors you have doubles with each generation. Go back to your great-great-great grandparents and you have thirty two. One more generation is sixty four. I could go on, but you get the point."

"That's a lot of relatives," David said.

"You're right," Harley agreed. "And that's only going back six generations. If you go back fifteen generations, to where you'd say the word great thirteen times before the word grandparent, guess how many ancestors you have?"

"I can't figure that out," David said.

"If he can't, I sure can't," I added.

"Well, lucky for y'all, I know the answer," Harley said. "Hope you're ready, because here goes. The number of ancestors you had fifteen generations ago is thirty two thousand seven hundred and sixty eight."

"Wait, what?" Will asked.

"Mind boggling, isn't it?" Harley said. "But it's true. And that's only going back a few hundred years. Keep going back even further, and you've got millions of ancestors."

"Why didn't I know that already?" I asked.

"Most people have no idea," Harley explained. "But here's what I'm trying to tell you. If you go back in your family tree you're going to find all kinds of people. Maybe some royalty, maybe some village idiots. So none of us are any better or any worse than anyone else. We're all put on this earth with the ability to direct our own lives. We can't let people tell us that our family, or any other circumstances we were born into, can stop us from the success that we control. Make sense?"

"Definitely," Brew said.

"Good," Harley said. "And I'll keep elaborating on everything I've already talked about. Now let's get out of here."

## CHAPTER NINETEEN

"How you doing, Harley?" Brew asked when we got to the top of the bleachers.

With a huge grin he answered, "I've got a warm bed, a roof over my head, and I'm always well fed. So what more needs to be said?"

We all cracked up. David even slightly applauded as he asked, "Did you make that one up too?"

"I guess I did," Harley answered.

"That's another good one," Will said.

"And another one I plan on using," I added.

"Well, feel free," Harley responded as he looked down at me before continuing. "In fact, anything I say at our weekly sessions is not only something I would not mind if you repeated, but I'd be flattered if you did."

"I'm definitely planning to," Brew said.

"Good," Harley responded. "Now what I said was me just trying to have a good attitude. And to be glad of what I have. Sometimes the little things in life are what we need to be the most thankful for. It all depends on your perspective."

"What do you mean?" David asked.

"Well, I'm glad you asked," Harley answered. "Because believe it or not, I've got a story to tell that gives a good example of just what I mean."

Of course Will had to make a sarcastic comment. "YOU'VE got a story?"

"Yes, I do, cheeky one," Harley answered.

Will smiled knowing that, once again, Harley had bested him. Then Harley continued. "A few years back, a group of Dowling students went on a camping trip up in the Virginia mountains. Several of them decided to go off hiking. After a mile or so they broke off and went in different directions. Two boys were determined they were going to make it the top of the highest mountain in that area. And they did. And when they got to the top, there was a big boulder. Even bigger than the rock I sat on when we met in the fall."

We all nodded as we followed along.

Harley continued. "Well, when they saw the boulder one of the boys sat on it, then took off his boots, looked at his foot and said, 'Look at those sores.' But the other boy climbed to the top of the boulder and said, 'Look at that view.' See the difference in their perspectives?"

"Absolutely," Brew said. "One complained about his sore feet, the other enjoyed the scenery."

"Exactly," Harley said. "They had both hiked the same distance, up the same mountain. And I'm sure their feet both hurt the same too. But the one boy chose to ignore the pain and enjoy the view. I guess he knew that he may never get up there again, so he needed to make the best of it."

"Interesting," I said.

"It is," Harley agreed. "I've told y'all before that life is short, and it's definitely too short to complain about things. Especially little things like that. Instead of complaining, enjoy!"

"True," David agreed.

Harley nodded as he went on. "Sometimes it may be hard to realize just how lucky we are. But we are. What we take for granted are things few people ever have. That's why you need to enjoy this world, because you won't be here but so long. In a nutshell, in life you need to ignore the sores on your feet and enjoy the scenery."

"Another good way of looking at things," I said.

"Thank you," Harley responded. "Now I'll leave on this. Just be thankful. Because right now there are billions of people on this earth praying for what you already have."

# CHAPTER TWENTY

At practice the next Monday Coach Samuels didn't like what he saw. I'm not sure what it was, but it was something. I guess he didn't think we were hustling enough. Whatever it was, the whole team had to stay after and run extra laps. A lot of them. We always had to run them before practice, but never after one.

By the time we got up to the top of the bleachers we were not only running late, but we were pretty much out of breath as well. Harley had seen what happened and was laughing really hard when we sat down. "I guess that'll teach y'all to practice hard every day," he said.

"I guess so," Brew said.

"Well, that's okay," Harley replied. "Today's lesson is probably my quickest one. I've been saving it for a day like today when we're a little short on time. So I won't waste any more time. You ready?"

"Sure," Will responded.

"Okay then," Harley said. "Remember in one of our first lessons when I told y'all not to put things off, and to start?"

"Yes, sir," David said.

"And what did I say that start stood for?" Harley asked.

We all hesitated for a second trying to remember. I had it on the tip of my tongue before Brewer beat me to it. "Stop talking and really try?" he asked. "Was that it?"

"That was it, exactly," Harley answered. "You make me proud, boy."

"I try," Brew replied.

Harley continued. "Well, I have another version of that. How do you spell the word now?"

We all waited to see who would say it first. Finally, I jumped in and answered, "N-O-W."

"Exactly again, "Harley said. "Y'all are on a roll today."

"Maybe those extra laps we had to run cleared our brains," I said.

"Well, whatever it is, it's working," Harley agreed.

"Just don't give Coach Samuels any ideas," Will said.

"Don't worry, I won't," Harley promised. "Okay, what does N-O-W stand for?"

"Now, as in now you're going to tell us, I hope," Brew said.

"I will," Harley said. "But this one is a little trickier. What are the first two letters in the word now?"

"N-O," David quickly answered.

"And what does that spell?" Harley asked, pointing at him.

"No," David replied.

"That's right," Harley said. "So the first two letters stand for no. Any idea what the letter W stands for? I'll give you a hint. It's goes with the theme of how you need to start and not put things off."

"I'll take a guess," I said. "Is it wait?"

"Close enough," Harley answered. "It's not wait, it's waiting. N-O-W stands for *No Waiting*. Simply put, it means don't wait around to get things started. Do them now. NO WAITING!"

"Pretty cool," Brew said.

"Of course," Harley went on. "But it's simple. Does

anybody like to wait? I mean wait for anything?"

"I don't," I said.

"Exactly," Harley agreed. "When you go to a restaurant, do you hope they'll tell you there's a long wait for a table? Or when you go to a movie, do you look forward to having to wait in line to buy a ticket? Or when you're flying somewhere do you hope your flight will be delayed? Of course not. I could go on with a million more examples, but y'all get the point. Nobody likes to wait for anything, but they sure like to wait to get things started. That's why I say now. As in do it now. NO WAITING. Got it?"

"We do," Will said.

"Good," Harley said. "Get out of here."

## CHAPTER TWENTY ONE

"Boys," Harley began the next week. "Y'all probably look at me and think I'm just the old maintenance man. But what would you think if I told you that you were looking at a millionaire?"

We all stared at him quietly, not sure what to say. Finally, David broke the silence. "Seriously?"

"Yep," Harley continued, "I am. And I don't mean that to sound braggy, but more to prove a point. That point being, if I can become a millionaire, anybody can."

We continued to stare, still amazed at what he was telling us. Then Brew asked, "How'd you do that?" I'm glad he asked it, because I was certainly wondering the same thing. David and Will probably were too.

"Well, that's the beauty of it," Harley answered. "Anybody can become wealthy in this country. And even though y'all will be heading off to some fine colleges next fall, that doesn't matter. Not to say you shouldn't get a good education, that's not what I mean at all. But what I do mean is that a lack of a good education doesn't mean you still can't end up with a lot of money. All you need is time. And that's why y'all are looking at a millionaire, and I'm looking at four future millionaires. Because of time."

"Time?" Will asked. "How's that gonna make us millionaires?"

"Because of a wonderful thing called compound interest," Harley answered. "In fact, I'm jealous of y'all because you have so much time on your hands."

"This ought to be good," I said.

"It is," Harley agreed. "You'll probably be twenty two when you graduate from college. So let's say you want to retire when you're sixty five. Maybe you won't want to retire then, but we'll use that as a good round number. Now, if you invest just a hundred dollars a month into a mutual fund, which as you may know is a collection of a bunch of stocks, and do that every month from age twenty two to sixty five, how much money do you think you'll have?"

"I don't know," Will said. "Fifty thousand. Maybe a little more."

"A whole lot more," Harley said. "Actually, you'd have over one million dollars. About one million and sixty five thousand to be exact."

"Excuse me, sir. What?" Brew asked.

"Crazy, isn't it?" Harley replied.

"But how do you know what kind of interest rate your investment is going to get?" David asked.

"Good question," Harley answered. "And you won't know for certain. But the stock market has averaged eleven percent a year for decades now, actually a little bit more. So that's the interest rate I'm going to use."

"Fair enough," I said.

"Now here's where it gets even more interesting," Harley continued. "Let's say you put off investing a few years out of college and wait until you're twenty five to start investing that hundred dollars a month. How much do you think you'd have at age sixty five by then?"

"If you'd have over a million by starting at age twenty two," Brew said, "I can't imagine waiting three years would make that big a difference. I'll guess right at a million exactly."

"Not even close," Harley said. "If you wait just three years you'll have just under seven hundred and seventy five thousand."

"Huh?" we all said together.

"Scary, isn't it," Harley continued. "Waiting just three years to begin investing, or thirty six hundred dollars out of your pocket, will cost you almost THREE HUNDRED THOUSAND DOLLARS!"

"How is that possible?" David asked.

"Again, it's because of time and compound interest," Harley said. "Compound interest is simply your money working for you. And the more time you have, the more it works for you. Now suppose you wait until age thirty to begin this. How much would you have at age sixty five then?"

"My mind is still boggled from that last one," I said. "So I won't dare guess."

"Well, I'll tell you," Harley said. "It's just under four hundred and fifty five thousand. So waiting just eight years to begin this will cost you over six hundred thousand dollars."

"Whoa," Will said.

"And it gets worse," Harley said. "Wait until age forty and you'll only end up with about one hundred fifty two thousand. I could go on, but I'm sure you get the point."

"My brain is ringing," Brew said.

"That's why I say that you're lucky you're young," Harley continued. "You've got time on your hands. So take advantage of it."

David raised his hand as he asked, "But, Harley,

when we're sixty five years old, won't a millon dollars, or even a little bit more, be worth a lot less than it is now because of inflation?"

"Good question," Harley answered. "And the answer is yes. Of course a million dollars won't be worth as much when y'all are sixty five as it is now. But you know what?"

"What?" David asked.

"A million dollars isn't worth as much now as it was forty years ago. But would y'all turn down a million dollars right now? Or ever, for that matter?"

"No," we all agreed as we laughed.

Harley continued. "Yeah, it's true that a million dollars doesn't buy as much today as it did forty years ago. And it won't buy as much in forty years as it does today. But what is also true is that a million dollars in cash always has been, and always will be, a lot of money. Forty years ago I'll bet some students sat at this very school and thought the same thing. But there are probably a lot of them that don't have a million dollars, or anywhere close to that today."

"Good point," Brewer said.

"I'm glad you think so," Harley smiled. "I've talked about how you have to start and do it now, right?"

"You have," I said.

"Well, this is another prime example," Harley said. "Only this time not starting and not doing it now will cost you a whole lot of money. I also talked about how people have a bad case of the somedays, remember?"

We all nodded our heads.

"Well, don't say that someday you'll start investing," he said. "Now, next week I'll talk a little bit more about this. Until then, boys."

## CHAPTER TWENTY TWO

"Okay, boys," Harley began. "Last week I said I'd talk about a little bit more about what we were discussing. We were talking about investing, right?"

"Yes, sir," I said. "Some of those figures are still blowing my mind."

"Good," Harley replied. "Because they are pretty crazy. But one thing that can hurt how much you invest is debt. Now, how many of you already have debt?"

We all looked around at each other before David answered with, "I don't think I do."

"Me, either," Brew said. Then Will and I nodded in agreement.

"That's good," Harley said. "Just like last week I said you're all lucky because you have time on your hands to invest. Well, you're lucky that you don't have any debt, either. Keep it that way!"

"But don't most people have debt?" I asked. "Most adults, anyway?"

"Yes, they do," Harley answered. "The large majority do. But that doesn't make it okay, because they probably have no idea how much money they are wasting and costing themselves in the long run."

"What do you mean?" David asked.

"Well, I'll put it this way," Harley answered. "Let's say you have a credit card that you owe ten thousand dollars on."

"Who would be dumb enough to do that?" Will asked.

Harley laughed before answering. "Who? Pretty much everybody. Only about ten percent of all Americans routinely pay their credit card bill in full every single month."

"Seriously," Will said. "I thought it was the other way around. That only a small percentage didn't pay them in full."

"Unfortunately, that's not the case," Harley said. "But maybe that assumption is because everybody thinks they are the only ones who aren't paying their cards off in full. They think they are in a small minority. But actually, they are in a large majority."

"Something else you're telling us that I never knew," Brew said.

"Well, now that you know that much, let me continue," Harley said. "So if you have a credit card that you owe ten thousand dollars on, and you're interest rate is twenty five percent, how much interest are you paying each year?"

"Twenty five percent of ten thousand?" David asked. "That would be twenty five hundred."

"Right," Harley said. "So if you're paying that amount in interest every year, how much is that over ten years?"

David was again the first one to chime in. "Twenty five thousand," he answered.

"You're right again," Harley said. "Twenty five thousand just in interest. Ridiculous, huh?"

"Definitely," Will said.

"It is," Harley agreed. "But what's crazy is that most people just pay what they can every month and know they're paying interest, but they never think about how much it adds up over the years. But let me take it even further."

"Do it," I said.

"Ok," Harley said. "Suppose you keep your credit card paid off in full every month. And suppose instead of paying twenty five hundred in interest every year, you invested that. After ten years, how much do you think you'd have?"

"I won't begin to guess," Brew said. "After what you told us last week, there's no telling."

"You'd have over forty five thousand dollars," Harley said. "Even though you've only put in twenty five thousand, you have accumulated nearly double that amount. So instead of paying twenty five thousand to the credit card company, you have over forty five thousand dollars. That's a seventy thousand dollar difference in your favor."

"Wow," was all I could say.

"But here's an even bigger wow," Harley continued. "Let's say you do the same for twenty years. Twenty years of investing twenty five hundred a year. Guess how much you have then?"

"Double the years," I said, "Then I guess you'd have double the amount. Ninety thousand, right?"

"That's what everybody assumes, but it's wrong," Harley told us. "Actually, you'd have over one hundred eighty thousand dollars. Even though the time you invested doubled, the amount of money you have quadrupled."

"That's amazing," David said.

"That's the beauty of compound interest," Harley agreed. "And that's why it's been called the eighth wonder of the world. And that's why it's important to let interest work for you instead of against you. In other words, interest should be made not paid."

"Sounds easy enough," Brew said.

"It is easy," Harley agreed. "But most people don't realize how easy it is. That's why they don't take advantage of it. And most people would rather buy stuff they can't afford on their credit card than invest. That's why, like I was telling you last week, most people end up with very little money in their old age."

"Stupid," Will said.

"Yep," Harley replied. "Next year when you get to college you're gonna be walking around campus during your first week, and you know what you'll see?"

"Girls, hopefully," Will said.

"Something we don't get to see too much around here," Brew added.

"Okay," Harley laughed as he spoke. "You'll see some girls. But what you'll also see will be tables with people trying to get you to sign up for a credit card. But just keep on walking."

"Why?" I asked.

"Think about it," Harley answered. "Most kids in college don't have jobs, so how are they going to pay for stuff they've bought on a credit card?"

"Good point," I said.

"And the credit card companies know this," Harley

said. "Sadly, that's why they do it. They want kids to get in debt to them. And that's why the average college student graduates with about four thousand dollars in credit card debt."

"They do?" Will asked.

"They sure do," Harley said. "And to make matters worse, over a million and a half Americans file for bankruptcy every year, and twenty percent of them are under the age of twenty three."

"What?" Brew asked.

"Scary, isn't it." Harley said. "And that's why you don't need a credit card in college. But when you get out of college and are, oh, I don't know….actually working, then you can get a credit card. But just one. Some people think it's a sign of success to have a bunch of credit cards, but it's not. Having more than one credit card is like having more than one girlfriend. It may seem cool, but eventually it'll catch up with you and you'll be in big trouble."

We all got a good laugh at that one.

"And when you do get that one credit card," Harley continued, "use it as little as possible. Only when you really must. I find that the less I use my credit card, the smaller the bill is. Funny how that works."

We all nodded our heads to let Harley know we understood.

"And when you get out of college and start working, be patient with how you spend your money," Harley said.

"How so?" Brew asked.

"Well," he went on. "Just don't go out and buy stuff you can't afford. There's nothing worse than someone who buys things they can't afford, just to make it look like they can afford them."

"Interesting," David said.

"It is," Harley agreed. "But don't get caught up in that trap. Too many young people buy cars and houses and join clubs they can't afford, just to keep up with people. The only problem is the people they're trying to keep up with are trying to keep up with them. It's a crazy cycle. Like the Bible says in Proverbs, 'Some who are poor pretend to be rich; others who are rich pretend to be poor.'"

"I didn't realize that went on," I said.

"It does," Harley said. "People want to buy things on credit when they're young, instead of waiting until they're older and can actually afford it. Don't fall into that trap. And another thing, when you're ready to get married, make sure whoever you marry is on the same page with you about this. Believe it or not, the number one thing that leads to divorce is money."

"Seriously?" Will asked.

"Seriously," Harley answered. "And there's not even a close second."

We all stared at him as he stared back at us in silence for several seconds. Finally, Harley continued. "Boys," he said. "You're so lucky. You've got time on your hands when it comes to investing. And now I'm sitting here looking at four young people who have no debt. KEEP IT THAT WAY! How do you spell debt?"

"D-E-B-T," David answered.

"And I bet you know what I'm about to ask next," Harley said.

"What's that stand for?" Will replied.

"And what does it stand for?" Harley asked.

"Not a clue," Will said.

"Well, here goes," Harley said. "D-E-B-T stands for *Don't Ever Begin This*. In other words, if you don't have debt, don't start now."

"Good advice," Brew said.

"It may be the most important thing I'll tell you all year," Harley said. "Now go get some dinner."

## CHAPTER TWENTY THREE

We were about two months into basketball season. So far it was going pretty well. A lot more wins than losses. A few games were huge blowouts, so I actually managed to get a little bit of playing time. I was that kid that every school basketball team had that rarely scored. But when I did, the gym went crazy.

We had gotten to a point where we really enjoyed our weekly sessions with Harley. We never knew what he was going to tell us each Monday, but we did know that it would be something good.

"Alright, boys," he began. "The last two weeks I've talked about finances, the dangers of debt and the importance of investing young. Today I'm going to tell you the beauty of both. Anybody care to guess what that is?"

"That you can retire comfortably?" Will asked.

"No, that's not it at all," Harley said. "Now when

you do have to retire, you want to be in a position where you can do that with no worries. But notice that I said have to retire, not want to retire."

"What's the difference?" Brew asked.

"Oh, there's a big difference," Harley answered. "If you have to retire, it just means you're getting older and maybe you're not up to working every day. But when you want to retire, that means you never really liked what you were doing to begin with, and that's kinda sad."

"Makes sense," I said.

"Look at me," Harley went on. "As I told y'all, I've got enough money to retire. But why should I? I love what I do and do what I love. If I retired I wouldn't know what to do all day. So I'm going to keep going while I still can."

"I hope I have that attitude with whatever I do," David said.

"You can," Harley replied. "Now obviously if you invest well, you'll be able to retire comfortably. But the beauty of staying out of debt and living below your means is that you'll have the freedom to do whatever it is that you want to do. Sometimes people do things they don't want to do and aren't really good at, just because they have a lot of bills to pay. If you ask them why they aren't living their dreams, or using the gifts that God gave them, they'll say it's because they can't afford to. But if you don't have debts, you can afford to do what you were put on this earth to do. You'll be able to take some risks or start your own business. You'll be able to live on less because you owe less. Do I make myself clear?"

"Definitely," Brew said.

"How many of you want to get a job when you get out of school?" Harley asked.

We all raised our hands quickly. But as fast as we raised them, Harley shook his head. "WRONG," he insisted.

"Huh?" we pretty much all replied together.

"Don't ever plan to have a job," he said.

"Why not?" I asked.

"I'll tell you why," he said. "But first, let me ask you this. How do you spell job?"

"Here we go," Will said. Then he answered, "J-O-B."

"Right," Harley responded. "Now what does that stand for?"

"I always thought it was something you did to make money," Brew said.

"It is," Harley said. "And that's not the way to go through life. Nobody wants to go through life doing something just because they get a paycheck. I know I don't. That's why I say J-O-B stands for *Just Outright Boring*. You don't want a job. A job is boring. What you want is a career. Something that you enjoy doing. See the difference?"

"I think so," David said.

"Then let me put it another way," Harley explained. "How do you spell career?"

"C-A-R-E-E-R," I answered.

"Good," Harley said as he smiled down at me from the top row of bleachers. "Now let me ask you this, Ben. What are the first four letters in that word?"

"C-A-R-E," I answered.

"You're not done yet," Harley almost shouted. "Now what does that spell?"

"Care," I replied.

"CARE," Harley said, now actually shouting. "Care. The first four letters in the word career are care. Do you think that's just a coincidence? NO! Because a career is something you're supposed to care about. It's something you should love doing. Not something you just go to every day. That's what a job is for. And nobody should have a job, you should all have a career."

A long pause came. We all sat speechless. What a

great analogy that was.

"Every year hundreds of Dowling alums come back for homecoming," Harley said, now almost in a whisper. "I try to talk to all of the ones that have been in school since I've been around here. And with all the years I've been here, that adds up to a lot of alums."

We all laughed. Brewer said, "I guess so."

"The reason I talk to them is because I want to know what they've been up to since graduating," Harley continued. "And let me tell you, nothing…and I mean NOTHING, makes me sadder than when someone is doing something that I can tell they don't love. It breaks my heart. They don't have a career, they have a job. And what's worse is that they may be really old before they realize how dumb that is. And then it may be too late to do anything about it. Because they're trapped into doing what they're doing, and they've racked up so much debt that they don't have any options. Don't do that, boys. Life is too short."

"Yes, it is" David said.

"It is, "Harley agreed. "And I'm going to hold you to that. I keep mentioning how you need to use the gifts that you were put on this earth with. Don't let them go to waste. The Good Lord didn't put you here to do that. He wants you to use them. He doesn't want you to do something just outright boring. He wants you to do something that you care about. Don't disappoint Him. Figure out what you were put on this earth to do, then do it. I'll end with this. Everyone is here to do something great, because life is too short to do something you hate."

He stood up and started walking down the bleachers. We got up to follow him, but he waved his hand back and forth for a second. "No, no," he said. "Don't leave. Not just yet, anyway. Sit here for a few seconds and think about what I just said. I bet if you think hard enough, you'll have some idea of what your gift is."

## CHAPTER TWENTY FOUR

Later that evening Brew, David, Will and I were drinking some coffee after dinner. There's an old saying that you know you went to boarding school if you've been addicted to coffee since age fifteen. That was no exception for the four of us. I tended to put way too much cream and sweetener in mine. A habit I never did break. I once had a teacher tell me that I might as well be drinking hot chocolate.

The break between dinner and study hall was one of the rare bits of free time that we got during the week. We tended to take advantage of that with a cup of coffee. More often than not, two cups. Sometimes other random students would join us. Occasionally even a faculty member or two. That night it was just the four of us. We always remained in the dining hall, usually the last ones to leave.

The dining hall was named for a man who had been the head cook there for over forty years. Maybe closer to fifty. I'd heard that he worked at Dowling longer than anyone else ever did.

Like the headmaster who the gym was named for, he had retired not long before I arrived, so I never knew him. Seeing the many buildings that were named for former employees of Dowling always gave me an idea of just how long the school had been there.

Just after we had all gone back for a second cup, Brew changed the subject from whatever random things we'd been talking about. "Harley was on fire tonight, huh?" he said.

"He certainly seemed really passionate about it, I'll say that much," I said.

"I've never really thought about finding your gift and doing something with it," David added. "I guess it makes life better if you're doing something that you really like."

"And that you feel like you were put on this earth to do," I replied.

"You know," Will said as he leaned up in his chair. "Not long ago I saw a story on TV. They showed a man in India who was in a pen with a bunch of cobras. About ten or twelve of them."

Brewer jumped in, "I saw that too."

"Yeah," Will continued, his Alabama accent getting thicker as it always did when he was telling a story. "They were surrounding him. And every time one got too close to him, he would smack them on top of their hoods. The one he'd just smacked would back away a little bit. But then another would come near him, so he'd smack that one too. They kept coming after him, but he just kept smacking them. It didn't seem to bother him."

"And then at the end of the story it said on the screen, do not attempt," Brew said. "As if I was going to if they hadn't told me not to."

"You couldn't pay me a million dollars to get in a pen with one cobra, much less a dozen," Will said. "And to smack them, at that? I don't think so."

"Me either," David said.

"But here's my point," Will continued. "He probably did it for very little money, maybe even no money. And not only did he not seem to mind doing it, he seemed to like it."

"What's your point?" I asked. "That he's a nut?"

"To us, maybe" Will answered. "But not to him. My point is, he found his gift. He knew he was put on this earth to handle snakes."

"I guess somebody has to," David said.

"Exactly," Will went on. "He was using his gift and doing something he loved. That was Harley's point today. We shouldn't waste our lives doing something that we don't love. Maybe we won't smack any cobras, but there's something deep down in all of us that we need to be doing."

"I don't think we'll find any cobras to smack. Not around here, anyway," I said. "But you're right."

"Maybe my gift is being right all the time," he responded with his trademark sarcastic smirk. "Too bad I can't make a living doing that."

"You'd be a billionaire by age thirty," Brew said. Then we took our last sips and headed to our dorm. As we walked outside the dining hall, I looked back over the front door to see the name of the man it was named for, and I couldn't help but realize something. Fifty years as the cook at the same place. If that's not using your gift I don't know what is.

# CHAPTER TWENTY FIVE

We managed to win the two basketball games we had since our last session with Harley. Usually our games were played on Tuesday and Friday nights. The game Friday night was on the road against a team that was said to be a lot better than us. But we won. Only by two points, but we were happy with it. Coach Samuels must have been happy too because he took it pretty easy on us in practice that day. Because of that, we got to the bleachers a little bit early. But Harley was already there. Knowing him, he knew practice would end a bit earlier that usual.

"I've talked a lot about living your dreams and using your gifts, haven't I?" he asked.

"Yes, sir," Brewer said.

"Maybe it's because I'm pretty passionate about it," he explained. "I think if everybody did what they were put on this earth to do, then everybody would be a lot happier. And God is too busy to put people on this earth to do something that doesn't make them happy. He's got better things to do. I think so, anyway."

"Probably so," David said.

"Indeed," Harley replied. "Last week I told y'all how it breaks my heart to see people come back for homecoming that are obviously not happy with what they're doing. Remember I said most of them have settled for a job instead having a career?"

"We remember," I said, assuming it was okay to speak for the other three.

"In all my years here, I've never met a kid who said they want to have a boring old job when they get out of school," Harley said. "Not one. But many of them do. I think it's because they decided to wish the wrong way."

"Wish?" David asked. "How do you wish the wrong way?"

"Well," Harley smirked. "Believe it or not, I'm glad you asked. Because I just happen to have the answer."

"I'm sure you do," Will said.

"And you'd be right," Harley responded. "And here goes. Whenever I see an alum that's not happy with what they're doing, I'm sure they are thinking that they wish they'd done something else. So how do you spell wish?"

"W-I-S-H," Brew answered.

"Good," Harley said. "Now what does that stand for?"

"No idea," I said. "But I'm sure you've got a good acronym for it."

"And once again, you would be absolutely right," Harley said. "W-I-S-H stands for *Well, I Should Have*. Because so many people sit around and wish that they'd done something different in their past. Which means they wish they were doing something different now. And they spend the rest of their lives thinking it's too late to do anything about it."

"Good one," David said.

"Thank you," Harley said. "And I'm glad you're realizing that while you're young. Now, here's another way to look at the word wish. W-I-S-H can also stand for *What If Success Happens?* See the difference?"

"Sort of," Brew said.

"Well, I'll explain it," Harley went on. "When you're old, you regret your past and say, 'Well I should have.' But when you are still young you can say, 'What if success happens?' In one case, you're regretting choices you've made in the past. In the other, you're realizing how much could still happen. And remember a while back I said that success is something YOU can control every single second. Do you see the difference?"

"Definitely," I said.

"Good," Harley said. "Because there's a big difference in the word wish. In a nutshell, don't say you wish you had, but instead wish for what you're going to do."

"We will," David said. This time he was the one speaking for all of us.

"Perfect," Harley said. "I'll end with this. As I said, I've seen tons of boys come through here and none of them wanted to do something boring with their lives. They all had big dreams. But most don't pursue those dreams. They get out of school and just don't even try. They think that pursuing their dreams is something that you just don't do as an adult. While they're here at Dowling they say, 'I want to be this or that,' and it's always something really cool. But then they don't do it. That's why I like to say, don't just say what you want to be, become what you want to be. In other words, turn your 'I want to be' into 'I am.' Don't say, 'I wish I had.' Instead say, 'I'm glad I did.'"

Like many times before, we were so overwhelmed by what Harley said we just sat in silence. He was silent too, then he got up and said, "Coach Samuels let you out of practice a little early, so I'll let you go a little early too. Enjoy your extra free time. And keep that winning streak going."

## CHAPTER TWENTY SIX

Harley began the next week as he had several times before by saying, "Alright, boys." It had become his signature opening. Then he continued. "I keep talking about living your dreams and using your gifts in life. I've said that too many people don't do that and then wonder why they're unhappy."

"Right," Brewer said.

"And like I said last week, they don't use their gift because they think grownups don't do that," Harley said. "But another big reason that so many people don't use their gift is because they're afraid they'll fail."

"Fail?" David asked.

"Yep," Harley answered. "Fail. Even though they know they have a gift for doing something, they think they're not really good enough to do it. But they are. Remember earlier in the year I talked about how no matter how good someone is at doing something, they all failed when they first tried it. That's why when I fail at something, I don't let it discourage me. I just feel like it's God's way of telling me to do something a little different. It's just a lesson in life. So I say the word fail stands for *Finding An Invaluable Lesson*. Remember what I told you the word gift stands for?"

"God is furnishing talent," I answered.

"Right," Harely said. "And what is the first word in that acronym?"

"God," we all said together.

"Exactly," Harley replied. "God. God is the one furnishing talent. Now if God is the one furnishing that talent, don't you think you're good enough to use it?"

"I guess if He thinks you're good enough, you are," David said.

"I'll put it this way," Harley went on. "If your coach put you in the game, you would never say, 'No, thanks. I'm not good enough.' Because you know if the coach thinks you're good enough, then you are."

"As little playing time as I get, the last thing I'm going to do is turn it down," I joked.

Everybody laughed, including Harley. Then he went on. "Or let me put it another way. If your classmates voted you to be president of your class, wouldn't you think that if they thought you could do it, you could?"

"Yes," Will said.

"Right," Harley said. "So if we agree with our coaches or our classmates that we can do what they think we can do, then why do we doubt what God is telling us we can do?"

"I've never thought about it like that," Brew said.

"Most people don't," Harley agreed. "But it's a good way to look at it. When you know you have a gift that you were put on this earth to do and you don't use that gift, it's almost like you're doubting God. I hate to put it that way, but it's true."

"That makes sense," Will said. "But why do people doubt what God wants them to do?"

"Like I said, they're worried that they'll fail," Harley said. "People don't have belief in themselves."

"Belief?" Brew asked.

"Yes," Harley answered. "And how do you spell that?"

"Belief?" I asked.

"Yes," Harley answered again. "How do you spell it?"

"B-E-L-I-E-F," I replied.

"Good," he said. "And B-E-L-I-E-F stands for

*Because Every Life Is Extremely Fantastic.*"

"Cool," David said.

"And it's true," Harley said. "Every life IS extremely fantastic. None of us were put on this earth to be any better than somebody else. You just have to have belief. Belief that you can do what God put you here to do. Or I'll put it another way. Has your mother or grandmother, or maybe an aunt ever made you cookies?"

"Oh, yeah," Will said.

"All the time," I added. "And they each think their cookies are the best."

"That's right," Harley said. "And they probably spend a lot of time making those cookies, don't they?"

"Yep," Will said. "But it only takes me a few seconds to eat them."

We all laughed for a moment before Harley jumped in. "Okay, okay," he said. "Now, let me ask you this. Are they proud of those cookies that they made?"

"Of course," Brew said.

"You mean," Harley said wide eyed, "they've never made a batch of cookies and said, 'Some of these are good and some of them are terrible.'"

"Why on earth would they make some that they

thought were terrible?" Will asked.

"Exactly," Harley replied. "Why on earth would they do that? The answer is, they wouldn't. They would never go to the trouble of making a bunch of cookies and thinking some were good and some were bad, would they."

"Of course not," David said.

"So," Harley continued. "If your mother or grandmother or aunt wouldn't go to the trouble of making bad cookies, why would The Good Lord go to the trouble of making bad people?"

"That's a good point," Brew said.

"Thanks," Harley said. "And I'm betting God is a lot busier in Heaven than your relatives are in the kitchen. But of all the billions of people he's created, there hasn't been one that He wasn't proud of. Not one that He didn't make for a reason. Not one that He looked at and said, 'This one's no good.'"

"But aren't there some bad people on this earth?" I asked.

"Of course," Harley replied. "And none of them are using their gift. Just use your gift, do what you know God put you here to do, and you'll be ok."

"Now," Harley said as he slapped his knees and stood to his feet. "All this talk of cookies has made me hungry."

## CHAPTER TWENTY SEVEN

A few days after that session we got our first snowfall of the year. Well, our first big one, anyway. I don't count a few flurries as a true snowfall. Like every part of the south, Virginia pretty much shut down at even a hint of snow. That is, unless you went to boarding school. Then it was business as usual. Nothing got cancelled.

Whenever it snowed at Dowling there was a tradition that had to be followed. After lunch and dinner, we were allowed to take trays from the dining hall and use them to sled down the hill overlooking the river. It was always fun to stand on top of the hill and look at the never-ending blanket of snow below, just before you slid down. We would attempt to race each other down the hill, but usually we just tried to make it to the bottom before tipping over or crashing. There's no telling how many trays were destroyed over the years, to a point where no one bothered to return them to the dining hall.

The next morning the snow had stopped falling, but there was still a huge amount on the ground. As Will and I were walking to our first class, I noticed two faculty members standing about ten or fifteen feet from us, talking to each other.

One was Mr. Roberts, the assistant headmaster and dean of students. He was from New Hampshire and had the accent to prove it. If you ever wanted to make him mad, just say something bad about his beloved Boston Red Sox. He was probably in his late thirties and had a thick beard that made him look like a Civil War general. He was talking to Mr. Daniels, the school athletic director, gym teacher and coach of the football and wrestling teams. Mr. Daniels was in his early thirties and had the frame to let you immediately know he was the coach of those teams. Big and solid with blonde hair and a matching mustache so thick that he was often compared to a walrus. I always assumed that he had played football somewhere before coaching it. The two of them seemed to pal around a lot. We even joked that Mr. Daniels was Mr. Roberts' bodyguard.

I picked some snow off the ground and rolled it into a ball. Then I looked at Will and asked, "Do you dare me?" Looking back, I don't know why I bothered with the question. Asking Will if he dared you to do something was like asking a dog if he wanted a piece of bacon. And met with equal enthusiasm at that.

"Okay, which one?" I asked.

"Mr. Roberts," he said.

I lobbed the snowball at him pretty softly, aiming for his back. Within seconds, I was reminded why I didn't pitch for the baseball team. My aim was not just a little off, it was over a foot too high. Yep, it hit him right in the back….of his head.

He turned around and looked to see who had been idiotic enough to do it. I guess my wide open mouth and eyes gave me away. But instead of coming after me, he snapped his fingers to get the attention of Mr. Daniels, then pointed to me and said, "Deal with him!"

Mr. Daniels started running towards me. I froze for a second, literally not sure what to do before I took off running. But even without the delay, it wouldn't have mattered. He caught me within a second or two, tackled me to the ground and rubbed some snow on my head, as dozens of students watched and laughed. Will being the one who laughed the hardest.

Mr. Daniels helped me to my feet, then asked, "Seriously? What were you thinking?" To this day I'm not sure of the answer.

Later that morning it dawned on me that this was another example of what Harley had been telling us. That you need friends to support you. Friends who will always be by your side. What better friend to have than one who will tackle a person in the snow, all because that person hit you with a snowball.

## CHAPTER TWENTY EIGHT

"So let me ask you boys something," Harley began the next week. "Have y'all ever heard of southern directions?"

"Are southern directions different than other directions?" Will asked.

"You bet they are," Harley answered. "In the south, you can't give directions without using the word yonder."

"I never thought about that, but I guess it's true," I said.

"It sure is," Harley agreed. "But exactly how long is yonder?"

"I have no idea," I said. "I guess it's not a specific distance."

"Oh, I'd have to disagree," Harley said. "There are

several degrees of yonder, and each one is a different length."

"This should be good," Will said.

"Okay," Harley said. "For starters, there's over yonder. That's usually something that's just on the other side of the room. 'Hand me that pencil, it's just over yonder.' Then there's around yonder. That's a block or two away. 'Let's walk there, it's just around yonder.'"

We all chuckled as we started to understand his point.

"Then there's down yonder," Harley continued. "That's maybe two or three miles away. 'We'd better drive, that's down yonder.' Then last is way yonder. That might be over in the next county. 'My friend Bob lives waaaayyyy yonder.'"

"That's so true," Brew said.

"Now," Harley went on. "Do you remember when you came here to Dowling on your first day as freshmen?"

"Of course," I answered. "I was terrified."

"Me too," David said.

"I'm sure you all were," Harley replied. "Matter of fact, I bet in all the years this school has been around there's never been a single kid that wasn't scared when he first came here."

"Probably so," Brew said.

"Yep," Harley agreed. "But that's not my point today. Now, when your parents were bringing you here on that first day, did they have a plan?"

"Sure," Will said. "The plan was to drop me off."

We all laughed, except for Harley, who kept a somewhat serious face. "Okay, but that's not what I mean," he said. "When you headed here, regardless of where you came from, did your father just start driving, or did he have a plan on how to get here?"

"I guess he knew what direction he needed to go to get here," David said.

"Right," Harley said. "Your fathers didn't just start driving and hope they'd get here. They knew what direction to go."

"Of course," Will said. "Otherwise we'd still be trying to get here."

"That's correct," Harley said. "You can't get somewhere if you don't have a plan. And that's not just true if you're driving somewhere. It's true if you're trying to get anywhere in life. You have to have a plan."

"Well, yeah," I said. "Isn't that obvious?"

"It should be," Harley agreed. "But most people

don't seem to have a plan. Oh, sure, they may say they want to end up somewhere. But they don't know how they're going to get there. That's why you have to have a plan."

We all looked up at him as he took one of his long pauses.

"Remember a while back when I told you that the reason people always think the book is better than the movie is because when they read the book, they get to direct it?" Harley asked.

We all nodded our heads.

"Do you remember my point with that?" he asked.

"That we can control our lives just like a director can control a movie," Brew answered.

"That's pretty much it," Harley said with a proud smile. "You're the ones who control your lives. And part of doing that is deciding where to go and knowing how to get there. Just like you fathers knew where they were going when they brought you here, you have to know where you're going in life. Because if you don't know where you're going, you probably won't get there."

"Yep," Will said.

"Or let me put it another way," Harley continued. "If you don't know where you're going, you're gonna end up exactly where you are."

"Another good one, Harley," I said. "You have a good way of putting things."

"Thank you," Harley replied. "And I still have plenty more. Until next Monday."

# CHAPTER TWENTY NINE

As usual, Harley was sitting on the top row of the bleachers with his Dowling cap resting on one knee. The four of us sat on the row below him.

"So last week we talked about how you have to know where you're going if you want to get there," Harley said.

"Right," David replied.

"I talked about how your fathers knew where they were going when they brought you here on your first day," Harley continued.

"Right again," Will said.

"Okay," Harley said. "But let me ask you this. When your fathers drove you here, did they look straight ahead or behind themselves?"

"Huh?" I asked.

"You heard me," Harley answered. "Did they look straight ahead or behind?"

"Straight ahead, of course," Brew said.

"Of course," Harley said with great enthusiasm. "Now why do you suppose they didn't look behind?"

"Because they would never have gotten us here," Will answered.

"Exactly," Harley said with even more enthusiasm. "If they had looked behind, they would never have gotten you here."

"Right," Will added.

"Well, boys," Harley smiled. "Life is much the same. You can't get where you're going if you're always looking behind. Think about it. It doesn't matter if you're driving a long way, or just walking a short distance."

"Kind of like the different yonders," I said.

"Pretty much," Harley agreed. "And just like life, yonder is always ahead of you, not behind. Too many times in life we let what happened in our past keep us from doing something we want to do. Or better yet, something we know we absolutely should be doing."

"I guess that's true," Brew said.

"It most definitely is," Harley said. "But you

shouldn't let what's happened in your past control your future. Some of the best ideas and brightest minds were crushed because of one thing...one little thing that happened in the past. Something that happened years ago and didn't matter. You can't do one single thing about your past, but you can do everything about your future. Forty eight hours ago yesterday was tomorrow. There's nothing you can do about that. But in forty eight hours tomorrow will be yesterday, and you can do something about that."

"I'd be lying if I said I've never let something that happened to me in the past bother me," I said.

"That's okay," Harley said. "Because I'm going to tell you how to fix that. I keep saying the word past a lot today. Now how do you spell past?"

"P-A-S-T," David was the first one to say.

"Thank you, young man," Harley said. "Do you have any clue what that stands for?"

We all shook our heads no, not having a clue.

"P-A-S-T," Harley said. "That stands for *Put Away Sabotaging Thoughts.*"

"Good one," I said.

"And it's an important one too," Harley replied. "Don't let anything you've done in the past stop you. Put those sabotaging thoughts away."

"Cool," Brew said. "You've done it again."

"Okay, then," Harley continued. "It's probably been a while, but do you remember studying the pioneers?"

"Sure," David said. "In elementary school."

"I knew it had been a while," Harley said. "But I bet you remember a lot about them. How they rode in covered wagons out west to make a new life for themselves."

"Yeah," I said. "They were pretty brave."

"Indeed, they were," Harley agreed. "But there's something you may not have been taught in school. These people packed up everything they owned to head out west, but what did they get to along the way?"

"What?" David asked.

"The Mississippi River," Harley answered. "And it's about a mile wide in many parts, even wider in others. But did they cross it on a bridge? Nope. There were no bridges over the Mississippi back then. So they had to put their wagons on a raft made out of logs, then make it across."

"Really?" Brew asked.

"They sure did," Harley said.

"That doesn't sound easy," Will said.

"Well, I wasn't there," Harley said with a grin. "But I'm betting you're right. But there was one other problem."

"What was that?" David asked.

"Well," Harley answered, "If you think pulling a wagon across a mile of water is hard, think about all the stuff they had in that wagon. So what do y'all suppose they did?"

"I'm not sure," I said.

"They had to leave some stuff behind," Harley said.

"Wow," David and Brew both said at about the same time.

"That's right," Harley went on. "In order to get across that river and move forward, they had to leave some stuff behind. Right there on the bank of the river. Do you know the point I'm about to make?"

"I think so," I said. "But tell us anyway."

"That life is much the same," Harley explained. "Sometimes you have to leave stuff behind to get where you're going."

"Makes sense," Brew said.

"Now," Harley went on. "Last week when I was talking about southern directions, I left out a part. Have you ever asked somebody for directions and they began by telling you about something that's no longer there?"

"I'm not sure what you mean," David said.

"Well, let me give you an example," Harley said. "Not long ago I got lost in a little town. I pulled over and asked a lady how to get to the highway. She asked, 'Do you know where Mike's Deli used to be?' I couldn't help but wonder how she expected me to know where one restaurant used to be if I didn't know where a whole highway still was."

That one made us laugh hard. "I've had that happen," Will said.

"Me too," Brew said as David and I nodded in agreement.

"Of course," Harley said. "We all have. And my point is that a person shouldn't expect you to get where you're going if they're telling you about a building that was there in the past. Well, life is much the same. You can't get where you're going based on what used to be. You have to go by what's there now. Forget about the past, just worry about the future."

We all nodded our heads as he stood up. "Now if you'll excuse me," he said as he walked down the bleachers. "I find it easier to walk ahead. The only thing that's behind me is that wall. And I can't get anywhere that way."

## CHAPTER THIRTY

"Alright, boys," Harley began. "I've been giving y'all a lot of advice this year and telling you how to live your life how you want it and to use your gifts. In a nutshell, how to achieve true success. Right?"

"You have," David said. "And it's been good."

"Thanks," Harley said. "I hope y'all have been getting a lot out of it."

"Yes, sir," Brew said.

"Good," Harley continued. "Not long ago I told you that one of the main reasons people don't use their gifts is because they're afraid that they'll fail."

"I remember that," Will said. "You told us that fail meant finding an invaluable lesson.

"True," Harley said. "But there's another word that keeps people from living their dreams, and that word also starts with the letter F. Know what that word is?"

"Not sure," I said.

"Well, I'll tell you," Harley said. "That one word is fear."

"Fear?" Brew asked.

"Yep," Harley said.

"Fear of what, exactly?" David asked.

"That's just it," Harley answered. "Nobody knows. All they do know is that their fears are holding them back."

"But they don't know what that fear is?" I asked.

"Nope," Harley answered. "Not really. They just know they're afraid of something. But I have a theory as to what most people are afraid of. Any guesses?"

We all looked around hoping that one of the others would know. After several seconds we looked back up at Harley to see what it was.

"Change," he said, looking at each of our faces. "Change is what most people fear."

"Changing what?" Brew asked.

"Good question," Harley replied. "And that's just it. They think they have to change a lot about their lives, but really they don't."

"Why not?" Will asked.

"Well, again that's just it," Harley said. "They don't have to change anything. They just think they do. Look, we all have something inside telling us what we need to do. That's the gift I keep talking about. The one that we all have but that few of us use."

"Right," David said.

"But, again, people have a fear of using that gift," Harley explained. "They think they have to make big changes to make that gift a reality. But they don't. Trust me, if you have a burning desire to do something, and we all do, then the ability to do it is already there. You don't have to change a thing. Just use what you already have. Don't let fears keep you from using your gifts."

"Makes sense as always," Brew said.

"Then let me ask you this," Harley said. "Fear is spelled F-E-A-R. Now what does that stand for?"

"No idea," David said.

"Fear stands for *Forget Everything And Resume*," Harley replied.

"Forget what?" Brew asked.

"Whatever it is that's stopping you," Harley

answered. "And usually it's nothing that big. Nothing to be afraid of at all. That's why I say just forget and resume."

"Resume what?" I asked.

"Resume on with your life and do whatever you were put here to do," he answered.

"Okay, I'm done for the week," Harley continued. "Now we have a decision to make. Basketball season is about over. Next week spring sports begin, and you're all playing lacrosse again this year. So where should we meet? How about in front of the gym? That way we can stand out there and talk. But since the weather will be getting warmer, I can take y'all around some weeks and show you some things. There are still a lot of places on this campus that I need to tell you about. Sound good?"

"Sure," we all said.

"Perfect," Harley said. "Then I'll see you in front of the gym next week."

He got up and hurried out of the gym before the four of us were even out of the bleachers. As we walked to the door, Brew said, "More places to show us around campus. This should be interesting."

And we could hardly wait.

## CHAPTER THIRTY ONE

Basketball season had ended. We finished tied for first in our conference for the regular season. In the conference tournament we made it to the finals against the team we had tied with and managed to beat them by three points in double overtime. That put us in the state playoffs where we were, unfortunately, defeated in the second round. Spring sports were now here.

As promised, Harley was waiting outside the gym when we arrived the next week. There was a bench outside of the gym. Harley, with his Dowling cap on since we were outside, was standing next to it as we walked up. "Have a seat, boys," he said pointing to the bench. "I'll stand up for two reasons. One, I won't take long. Two, it will make me feel like I'm preaching to y'all. I don't know if I've mentioned it or not, but sometimes I fill in for the pastor at my church."

We didn't know that, but somehow it didn't surprise us. Not in the least.

"Have you ever heard the joke that starts, what are a redneck's last words?" Harley asked us.

"I think so," Brew said. "It's something like, 'Hey, y'all, watch this.'"

"Oh, yeah, I've heard that one," Will said as David and I nodded our heads and laughed.

"Okay," Harley said. "Well, I have a theory. Are you ready?"

"Sure," David said.

"Alright then," Harley said. "What would you think if I told you that the Wright brothers were rednecks?"

"The Wright brothers? Are you serious?" Brew asked.

"I absolutely am," Harley said. "Think about it. Here were these two brothers who owned a bicycle shop in Dayton, Ohio. Then one day they said they were going down to the Outer Banks of North Carolina to fly in a machine they had built. Now don't you know their friends and family though they were crazy?"

"Probably," I said. "But how does that make them rednecks?"

"Because just like the rednecks in that joke, they were doing something that was maybe kind of nuts," Harley said. "And maybe something that could have killed them. But did that stop them?"

"No," Will said.

"Exactly," Harley said. "They took a risk and did something crazy. But now, because they did, traveling has been a lot easier."

"That's true," David said.

"Okay, let me give you some more examples," Harley said. "This morning at breakfast, did you have any eggs?"

We nodded our heads that we did.

"How about milk?" Harley asked. "Did you drink any?"

David and Will nodded that they had.

"But have you ever thought about who on earth was the first person to try those things?" Harley asked.

"Not really," I answered.

"Well, it was probably somebody that might have been called a redneck," Harley said. "Years and years ago, who was the first person to try eggs and milk? Can't you see some guys on a farm saying, 'I dare you to eat that oval shaped white thing that the chicken just dropped.' Then the other one said, 'Well, okay. But only if you drink the white stuff we squeezed out of the cow this morning.' Do you see what I mean?"

"I never thought about who the first person was to

do that," David said. "But I guess people did think they were crazy."

"Of course they did," Harley said. "But if they hadn't done that, we would be pretty hungry every morning. And every food we eat and take for granted was first eaten by somebody. Every vegetable from the ground and every fruit from a tree. Even that coffee that I know y'all love so much. Somebody came up with the idea to put those beans in with some hot water and drink it."

"How'd you know we like coff…..never mind," Will said. "You know everything that goes on here."

Harley just laughed as he continued. "And it's not just food. Everything you have is because somebody took a risk when they invented it. Everything you do, somebody did first. Every book you read, every movie you see, everything you own and do is because somebody took a risk. And I can guarantee you one thing. Know what it is?"

"What?" I asked.

"That every one of those people were laughed at," Harley answered. "Maybe not to their faces, but definitely behind their backs. I bet even Thomas Edison had friends who said, 'I know a guy named Thomas. He's trying to invent something that will put lights in every house and building in the world. Yeah, like that's possible.'"

"Probably so," Brew said.

"You know it is," Harley agreed. "But the only thing worse than people who make fun of those who try, are people who never try themselves."

"Wow," David said.

And here's my point. Think of all we have and do that is because somebody ignored the laughs and criticism and took a risk. That's why I want every one of you to take risks too. Who knows what might happen if you do. Sure, you might fail at some things you try. But it's better to try and fail, than to not try at all."

"Good point, Harley," I said.

"It is if I do say so myself," Harley said. "Same time and place next week."

# CHAPTER THIRTY TWO

Just as Harley was about to start speaking the next week, he took off his cap and swatted at a bug that was buzzing near him. "Bugs can be annoying, can't they?" he asked.

"Pretty much," Will said.

"You know, that reminds me of something," Harley said. "A few years ago my family was at Virginia Beach. We'd been sitting out by the ocean for a while, when a bunch of bugs started flying around us. We tried swatting at them, but they wouldn't leave. It was annoying. So you know what we did?"

"What?" David asked.

"We got up and moved to a different spot," Harley answered. "One where there were no bugs. And we enjoyed the rest of the day. Sound simple?"

"Of course," Brew said.

"And it was simple," Harley agreed. "Nobody would be dumb enough to sit around while bugs were bothering them, now would they?"

"I hope not," Will said. "That would definitely be dumb."

"It would," Harley said. "But why is it that when bugs are bothering us, we leave. But when people are bothering us, we stay right where we are?"

"We do?" I asked.

"Probably," Harley said. "Have you ever had anybody in your life that bugged you but you did nothing about it?"

"I guess so," David said.

"We all have," Harley said. "But you have to move away from the bugs AND the people who bug you. Remember last week I talked about how everybody who ever did something great probably had people who made fun of them."

"Yes," we all said.

"Well, like I said, those people ignored the laughs and did what they knew was a good thing," Harley explained. "In other words, they moved away from the bugs."

"Ohhhh," David said. "That's true."

"It is," Harley said. "And some people just like to be a bug on your day at the beach. They see you trying to take a risk and attempting to do something great, and they laugh at you. Or even flat out tell you that you're crazy and can't do it. But when they tell you that you CAN'T do something, what they really mean is that they don't WANT you to do it."

"Why is that?" I asked.

"Probably because they're scared to take risks and do something great themselves, so they don't want you to do something great," Harley said. "They're holding themselves back, so they want to hold you back too. But if you keep hanging out with people who tell you what you can't do, basically you're agreeing with them. What you've got to do is get away from them. Just like my family moved away from the bugs, you've got to move away from the people that bug you. You've got to get up, walk away, and do what you need to do."

"I will," Brew said.

"Good," Harley said. "I hope so. Because just like bugs have ruined a lot of days at the beach, people that bug have ruined a lot of great ideas and dreams. And kept people from using their gifts that I keep talking about. So I'll leave you with this. When somebody laughs at you or tries to talk you out of doing what you know you were put on this earth to do, just tell them this. If you choose to be negative that's up to you, but please don't tell me what I can't do."

## CHAPTER THIRTY THREE

When we walked up to the front of the gym the next Monday, Harley was leaning over petting a dog.

"Is that your dog?" I asked.

"Nope," Harley said. "No idea who it belongs to. He just came up to me a minute ago."

That wasn't uncommon at Dowling. There were a lot of dogs wandering around. Most belonged to faculty members, some seemed to belong to no one in particular. But if you were a dog that didn't belong to anyone, Dowling was a great place to be. They always got plenty of attention and were well fed. Mr. Clifford was even known to carry dog biscuits in his pocket to pass out to any dog that came along.

Harley stopped petting the dog, but instead of walking away, the dog just sat in the grass. Maybe he wanted to hear what Harley had to say too.

"Boys, have you ever wondered why a lot of people keep dogs as pets?" Harley asked.

"Because they're nice?" David asked.

"Well, that's one reason," Harley agreed. "But why are they nice?"

"I've never thought about it," I said. "I just know that they are."

"True," Harley said. "But why don't people keep lions as pets?"

"Because they're not nice," Will said.

"That's true too," Harley said. "But maybe they could be."

"What do you mean?" Brew asked.

"I'm not sure how long people have been keeping dogs as pets," Harley said. "A long, long time, I guess. But maybe dogs are nice because people took them in as pets, fed them, loved them and gave them a good home. Maybe if years ago someone had taken in a lion as a pet, then fed it, loved it and gave it a good home, they might be nice too."

"I don't think I'd want a lion as a pet," David said.

"I know," Harley said. "But my point is that people are like animals. The better we treat them, the nicer they are to us. And the nicer someone treats us, the nicer we are to them in return."

"That's true," Brew said.

"Let me ask you this," Harley continued. "When was the last time you paid someone a compliment?"

"I'm not really sure," I said.

"Well, it should be something you can remember easily," Harley said. "Because paying a compliment is something you need to do at least once a day. Maybe not always to someone you know, it could be a stranger."

"We should?" Will asked.

"Absolutely," Harley insisted. "We might all be quick to complain about something, but when was the last time you went out of your way to praise someone, even for just a little something?"

"I hate to admit it," I said. "But again, I'd have to say I'm not really sure."

"That's okay," Harley said. "Just start doing it. I'll put it this way. Have you ever been in a restaurant where the food wasn't very good, so you complained to the manager about it?"

"I guess so," Brew said as the rest of us nodded in agreement.

"Okay," Harley said. "But have you ever been in a restaurant where the food was really good?"

"Sure," Will said.

"All the time," Brew added.

"Right," Harley said. "But did you tell the manager that?"

We all looked at each other before Brew answered, "I guess not."

"Few people do," Harley said. "It's funny, we might stand in line at a customer service counter for an hour to complain about something. But most people won't stand in line for five minutes at that same counter to pay a compliment."

"I've never thought about that," David said. "But it's true."

"It is true," Harley said. "People don't always pay compliments, but they should. The world would be a much better place if we all complimented more and complained less."

"It probably would," Brew said.

"Yep," Harley said. "I'm going to quote the Bible from Proverbs again. 'An encouraging word cheers a person up.' Let me give y'all an example. There's a diner down the road where my wife and I eat almost every Saturday morning. A lot of times we get the same waitress. Well, a while back as we were leaving, I told her that I loved when she waited on us because she always did such a great job. Then she started crying."

"Why was she crying?" Brew asked.

"That's what I wanted to know," Harley answered. "And when I asked her, she explained that earlier that morning another customer had told her she was the worst waitress he'd ever seen. Simply because his eggs were a little overcooked. She said that he had even made her cry and that she was having the worst morning because of it. But my simple little compliment changed her day entirely. She was crying again, but this time the tears were for a different reason."

"What a cool story," David said. "And I bet that made you feel good too."

"Of course it did," Harley said. "And I'm not just talking about complimenting people in places where you're a customer. When you get older and start your careers, and notice I said careers and not jobs, you might have bosses that are quick to criticize what you're doing. But they rarely, if ever, will go out of their way to compliment something you're doing. But they should."

"Bosses are bossy," Will said.

"They can be," Harley said covering up a laugh. "But when you all become the boss, I want you to promise me you'll give a lot more compliments than complaints. Go out of your way to let someone know they're doing a good job. When someone says, 'The boss wants to see you in his office,' let that be a good thing instead of a bad thing. It's just as easy to call someone in and tell them they're doing a good job as it is to tell them they did something wrong."

"That's true," David said.

"Yep," Harley agreed. "Remember last week I talked about how some people are going to tell you what you can't do and try to crush your dreams?"

"Sure," Brew was the first to answer.

"Well, sometimes it's hard to tell who's trying to criticize you and who's trying to compliment you," Harley said. "So here's a little test. Fill in the blank. 'If everyone treated me the way blank does, I'd be the happiest and most confident person in the world. But if everybody treated me the way blank does, I'd be the unhappiest and least confident person in the world.'"

"Got it," David said.

"Okay, but I'm not done," Harley said. "It may also be hard to tell if we're the ones who truly criticize or compliment. So take that test again. 'If I treated everyone the way I treat blank, I'd be the most loved person there is. But if I treated everyone the way I treat blank, I'd be the most hated person there is.'"

"That's got me thinking," I said.

"Good," Harley said. "That's the idea. Go through life and pay a compliment every day. Maybe even two. When you get married, tell your wife how pretty she looks, or how good something she cooked is, or just how much you love her. Tell your kids how proud of them you are. Even if you repeat a lot of the same compliments over and over, that's okay. Nobody gets tired of hearing a compliment. There's not an employee in the world who gets tired of hearing that they're doing a great job. There's also not a person in the world who will get tired of their spouse telling them how much they appreciate everything they do for them. Try it. I bet even the greatest singer in the world never gets tired of being told what a great voice they have."

"We will," I said as the other three nodded along.

"Good," Harley said. "So I guess y'all are heading to dinner now."

"Yes, sir," Brew said.

"Well, if the food is as good as it always is," Harley said, "let the cooks know how much you enjoyed it."

And that night we did just that. The cooks all seemed so appreciative, that we did it every meal for the rest of the year. And I bet they never got tired of hearing it.

## CHAPTER THIRTY FOUR

Harley wasn't standing near the bench the next week. Instead, he was sitting in the school pickup truck with a big smile on his face. As soon as we saw him, we smiled too. We know that he was taking us somewhere.

"I assume we're supposed to hop in," Will said as he somehow slipped into the front seat while the rest of us climbed in the back.

Harley drove us down the road that went to the river, then slowed down about halfway before pulling over to the side. "Climb on out, boys," he said. So we did just that.

Just a few feet from where he'd parked, the school had just started building a new complex for faculty housing. All that was there so far was a huge rectangular shaped hole for the foundation. It was maybe about six feet deep, and very even on the sides.

"Alright, y'all, jump in," Harley said.

"Jump in where?" I asked.

"In there," Harley said as he pointed to the giant hole.

Will was about to make a sarcastic comment, but then stopped himself. We just all jumped down into the hole knowing that Harley had a reason for it.

"Okay," Harley said as he looked down on us from the edge. "Come on out."

"How are we supposed to do that?" Will asked, this time not stopping himself from a sarcastic comment.

"Oh, you need some help?" Harley asked. "Hang on, I've got something for that."

He then returned to the truck and grabbed something out of the back of it. We watched him as he walked towards us and saw that he had a shovel in his hand. "Here you go," he said as he tried to hand it down to us.

"What good is a shovel going to do?" I asked.

Harley stood there for a few seconds staring at the shovel in his hand. "Hmm," he said. "You're right, I guess this won't do you any good. Hang on."

He walked back to the truck, then returned with an even bigger shovel in his hand. "My apologies," he said. "This should do it."

"I don't think so," Brew said.

"Oh, I guess you're right," Harley agreed. "Wait right there."

Once again, he walked back to the truck. This time he came back with a small ladder. "This ought to do the trick," he said.

And he was right. David, being the tallest, grabbed the ladder from him, then leaned it on the side of the hole and climbed out. The rest of us followed and then pulled the ladder up and put it back in the truck.

"What'd you learn today?" Harley asked.

"Not exactly sure," Will answered.

"Well, it's pretty simple," Harley explained. "In life, sometimes you'll find yourself in a hole. But do you need a shovel to get out of that hole?"

"No," we all said at about the same time.

"Of course not," Harley said. "If you're in a hole, a shovel is only going to get you in deeper. So do you need a bigger shovel?"

"No," we all said again.

"Right," Harley agreed. "If a shovel is going to get you into the hole deeper, a bigger shovel will only get you in that hole even deeper than that. So what was it that finally got you out of that hole, boys?"

"The ladder," Brew said.

"Exactly," Harley said. "The ladder got you out. If you're in a hole, don't keep digging with a shovel. And definitely don't keep digging with an even bigger shovel. Grab a ladder and climb out. It's simple, isn't it?"

"Sure," David said.

"It may sound simple," Harley said. "But you'd be surprised at how many people find themselves in a hole, then keep digging and digging and wondering why they can't get out. In a nutshell, life is much the same. It's easier if you put down the shovel and grab a ladder."

We all nodded to let him know that we got it.

"Now you may be wondering why I didn't just tell you that outside of the gym instead of bringing you here," Harley said.

"It did cross my mind," Will said.

"Fair enough," Harley said. "But isn't it better to experience an example instead of just being told about it?"

"I guess so," Will agreed.

"Exactly," Harley said. "Now get back in the truck. We've got a long thirty second ride back to your dorm."

## CHAPTER THIRTY FIVE

The next week Harley was waiting by the bench outside of the gym. No truck in sight. No field trip today, we assumed.

"Boys, has anything ever happened to you that made you mad?" Harley asked.

"Of course," we all said as we sat down.

"Can you remember exactly what it was?" he asked again.

"Too many things to remember," I said.

"Maybe," Harley said. "Or maybe you don't remember them because it was nothing to really remember."

I guess the blank look on our faces let Harley know that we weren't quite following him, so he continued. "We all get upset sometimes, but most of the time, it's over something really silly that doesn't matter and that wasn't worth getting mad about in the first place. Think about how many times something seemed worth getting upset over, then later you realized it wasn't anything worth getting upset over at all."

"Like what?" David asked.

"Okay," Harley said. "Maybe your car won't start. Maybe you're late for something. Maybe you realize that the shirt you were planning on wearing has a stain. Maybe you drop and break something. I could go on and on, but you get the point. It may seem like a big deal now. But in a week, or tomorrow, or even in five minutes, you'll realize it wasn't that big of a deal at all. Then you'll feel like a fool that you got so mad in the first place."

"I guess I do that all the time," Will said.

"We all do," I added.

"We all stress over stupid stuff that isn't worth stressing over," Harley said. "And speaking of stress, how do you spell it?"

"S-T-R-E-S-S," David said.

"Right," Harley said. "And rather than ask y'all what that might stand for, I'll just go ahead and tell you. S-T-R-E-S-S stands for *Sweating To Really Extremely Silly Stuff.* And believe me, everything we stress about is silly stuff. It may not always seem silly at the time. But later you'll realize that it was."

"Probably so," Brew said.

"Not probably," Harley said. "Definitely."

"You're right," Brew said. "My apologies, sir"

"No need to apologize," Harley said. "Or should I say, don't sweat it."

We all laughed while he walked away. As we headed back to our dorm, Will said, "You know, all these years I thought Harley was the maintenance man. But maybe we should call him the acronym man."

## CHAPTER THIRTY SIX

The next Monday Harley was waiting in the truck when we arrived. There were several trucks that belonged to the school, but for some reason he always seemed to be driving the same one. Maybe it was because he had the seat adjusted just how he liked it. This time I managed to ride shotgun.

He drove us to one of the edges of campus where we rarely went, pulled over to the side of the road and told us to hop out. He walked to the front of the truck, then pointed to some land just across a tall white wooden fence. The fence that seemed to completely border Dowling, except for the part where the river was our border. "What do y'all see over there?" Harley asked.

"A farm?" Brew asked, seeming not too sure if it was the right answer.

"That's right," Harley assured him. "And what do they grow over there?"

We couldn't see it very well over the fence, so Will took a shot. "Since this is Virginia, I'm guessing tobacco."

"That's right, it is tobacco," Harley said. "Now why do you reckon there's no corn in that field?"

"Because they planted tobacco," David said.

We all laughed as Will said, "Well, that's a pretty obvious guess."

"It may be a pretty obvious guess," Harley said. "But he's also completely right."

"See!" David said to Will.

We all laughed again before Harley held up his hand to stop us. "The reason there's never any corn in that field is, indeed, because this farmer planted tobacco," he said. "But do you think there was ever a morning when he woke up, walked out to his field, then looked around and wondered why he didn't have any corn?"

"I hope not," Brew said. "Or he'd be pretty disappointed."

"That's right," Harley agreed. "But he wouldn't just be disappointed, he'd be pretty crazy too. Why on earth would he expect to have corn if he planted tobacco?"

"Of course," I said.

"Well," Harley said. "Just like with a lot of other

things I've told you this year, life is much the same."

"How so?" David asked.

"I touched on this a while back," Harley said. "If you didn't study for a test, would you expect to get an A?"

"No, Sir," Brew said.

"I've tried that a few times," Will joked. "It never works."

"Of course not," Harley said. "And like I also mentioned before, would you expect to win a game if you never practiced?"

"Probably not," I said.

"And that's something our coaches would NOT let us try," Will added.

"Well, there you go," Harley said. "That's my point. If you don't study, you won't get a good grade. If you don't practice, you won't win the game. And if you don't plant something, you can't expect to grow it. This farmer didn't plant corn, so he didn't expect to grow any corn. But he did plant tobacco, and in return he got acres and acres of it. So don't expect things in life if you're not willing to do your part first. In other words, just like the Bible says in Galatians, 'You reap what you sow.'"

"Good lesson," David said.

"Thank you," Harley replied. "And I hope that actually bringing you out here and showing this farm to you, made for a better example."

"It did," Brew said. "Thanks."

## CHAPTER THIRTY SEVEN

We had barely sat down on the bench the next week before Harley jumped into it. "Boys," he said. "I've talked a lot this year about not putting things off, have I not?"

"Yes," we all said together.

"Does anyone remember what I told you that the word start stands for?" he asked.

"Stop talking and really try," Will said.

"Good," Harley said as he nodded and smiled in his direction. "How about the word now, what did I say it stands for?"

"No waiting," Brew said.

"Y'all make me proud" Harley said. "And what does the word T-O-O stand for?"

"Talked out of," I said.

"Exactly," Harley replied. "And I even talked about how to not have a bad case of the somedays. You can't put things off, because then by the time you get around to doing it, somebody else may have beaten you to it. Y'all remember that I talked about how people probably thought the Wright brothers were crazy? Well, even though some people laughed at them, there were probably many others who claimed to have had the same idea. Maybe they did, maybe they didn't. But if they did, someone beat them to it. And they spent the rest of their lives regretting that they put it off."

"Makes sense," David said.

"Yep," Harley said. "You know, whenever my wife and I are about to go out to dinner and I ask her where she wants to go, she always says, 'It's up to you.' Never once in all the years we've been married has she said the name of an actual restaurant. Nope. She just says, 'It's up to you.'"

"My mom does that too," Will said.

"I think the reason people say, 'It's up to you' is because they don't want to be the one to decide where to go," Harley explained. "They don't want to make the decision. Well, life is much the same. Sometimes we don't make decisions simply because we're afraid of making the wrong decisions. We keep putting it off and putting it off. So don't put things off. Because if you don't do it, someone else will. Now don't put off getting to dinner. I'll see y'all next week."

As we were walking back to the dorm we passed by the school chapel, one of the oldest buildings on campus and also the prettiest. The original building on campus was a large one that was not only a dorm, but also had some classrooms and the office. Now it served as just the administration building. The chapel came along shortly after that.

The school chaplain, Father Edwards, was outside watering some flowers that lined the brick path going to the front door. As always, he was wearing his white collar. He was probably in his early sixties, if I had to guess. He had white hair left only on the sides of his head, along with a short white beard that always seemed to be perfectly trimmed. Everyone on campus was very fond of him. But no one called him Father Edwards. Everyone just simply called him "Preacher."

Preacher was widowed fairly young and never remarried or had children. I think we were his children. If any alums came back to the school for a visit, they most always stayed in his house. Those who did would find a silver service set with coffee and cookies at the foot of their bed when they came back in the guest room from the shower. To say he was he was very prim and proper was an understatement. He spoke so poetically that you might think he was British. But he was a born and bred Virginian. I once heard from a pretty reliable source that he came from a very wealthy family. But upon inheriting his share, he gave it all away. Obviously, he was a true man of God.

"Hi, Preacher," we all said.

"Hello, lads," he said. "I see you've been chosen this year."

It seemed like someone else had said that to us back in the fall. "Excuse me, sir," Brew said. "Chosen for what, exactly?"

"You shall see," Preacher said.

"We shall see what?" Will asked.

"We shall see each other at chapel on Sunday," Preacher said as he turned and walked inside.

## CHAPTER THIRTY EIGHT

"It looks like we're going somewhere today," Will said, as we noticed Harley sitting in the truck. It was such a nice spring day, we all jumped in the back to enjoy the breeze as we rode along.

Harley took us the short distance to the school's outdoor pool. As soon as he put the truck in park, we hopped out.

"Come on over here, boys," Harley said as he walked over to the pool and leaned on the gate that bordered it. He then pointed over to the pool. "How many diving boards do you see?" he asked, pointing towards them.

"Two," we all said.

"Right," Harley replied. "Two. Now do you notice anything different between those two diving boards?"

"One's taller than the other," I said.

"Well, duh," Will replied.

Before we had a chance to laugh a little, Harley cut in. "It is pretty obvious," he said. "Because one is only about three feet off the water, and the other is about fifteen feet up. So if you were trying to make the biggest splash that you could, which one would you jump from?"

"The taller one," I answered, before turning to Will and saying, "And don't say, 'Well, duh.'"

"That's also pretty obvious," Harley said. "If you want to make the biggest splash, you have to jump off the highest diving board."

"Sure," David said.

"Okay," Harley continued. "But if you want to make a big splash from the highest diving board, what do you have to do first?"

"Climb up it," Brew said.

"Exactly," Harley said. "You have to climb up the ladder. Now which board has the highest ladder to climb?"

"The tallest one," Brew answered again.

"Right," Harley replied. "Of course! The tallest one is going to have the highest ladder. In order to get to the highest diving board, you have to climb the highest ladder. But is it worth it?"

"Sure, it is," David said.

"That's right," Harley said as he slapped his hands together with excitement. "And life is much the same. If you want to make the biggest splash, the first thing you have to do is climb the biggest ladder. You follow me?"

We all nodded our heads.

"Good," Harley said. "Now follow me to the truck so I can take you back to your dorm."

# CHAPTER THIRTY NINE

"Nope, don't sit down," Harley said to us the next Monday as we were about to plop down on the bench. "We're going on a little trip."

"But where's the truck?" David asked.

"No need for the truck," Harley explained. "It's just a short walk."

And it was a short walk. Maybe a hundred yards over to the school's auditorium. It was named for an alum that was not exactly a household name, but who had won two Tony Awards for his work on the Broadway stage many years ago.

It was weird walking into the back of that auditorium when it was empty. It seemed so much smaller and less intimidating than when you were standing on its stage. I had done that in a few plays, as well as in my recent senior speech. Something all Dowling students are required to give near the end of their final year. Just a short one, talking about their memories of the school.

We followed Harley as he walked down the aisle, then stopped in front of the stage and turned to look back at us. "You know, boys, I've seen a lot of performances in this place," he said in a loud whisper. "Plays, concerts, speeches. Some good, some…..well, maybe not as good."

We all giggled softly as Will said, "I've seen some of those too."

"Okay," Harley said. "Get up on the stage."

"All of us?" I asked.

"Yes, all of you," he answered.

As usual, we weren't sure where he was going with this. But we walked up the stairs on the side of the stage, then walked down to the stage front.

"Look around," Harley said, still standing at the bottom of the stage. "It's cool, isn't it? Shakespeare once said, 'All the world's a stage.' I think that's true. But I'll add this to what he said. All the world's a stage. So go out in life and get all the standing ovations you can."

With that, Harley turned and walked away. We all stayed on the stage for a minute in dead silence, soaking it all in. Perhaps wondering where in life our standing ovations would come from.

## CHAPTER FORTY

The next week Harley was sitting in his truck. "We're not going very far this week, either, boys," he said. "But hop in anyway."

We drove down to the side of the road next to the hill where our weekly lessons began. The hill overlooking the river. We walked up to it. Then Harley sat on his rock and patted it a few times, almost as if it were an old friend.

"Well, boys, the year is almost over," Harley said. "We've got time for one more meeting after this week. Then you'll start your final exams. And what comes right after final exams?"

"Celebrating," Will said.

"Okay," Harley agreed. "Fair enough. But that's not what I meant. What event comes after exams? Right before graduation?"

"Are you talking about the awards ceremony?" David asked.

"Yes, I am," Harley said. "Now, how many of you expect to get some of those academic awards?"

"I'm not really sure," I said. "Probably none for me."

"Or me," Will said.

"Wait," Harley said. "You mean you don't expect to get the award for the highest GPA?"

"Hardly," Will said as I shook my head in agreement.

"And why don't you expect to get that award?" Harley asked.

"Because I didn't have the highest GPA," I answered. This time Will shook his head in agreement.

"So you mean just because you didn't get the highest GPA, they won't give you the award for it?" Harley asked.

"Of course not," I said.

"Exactly," Harley said. "So when they're about to announce the winner of that award, you won't be getting ready to stand up?"

"I guess not," I answered.

"Where are you going with this one?" Will asked.

"I'll tell you," Harley replied. "You wouldn't expect to win the award for the highest GPA if you didn't get the highest GPA, would you? Well, once again I'm about to say this. Life is much the same. You can't expect to get something that you didn't work for. In this case, the award for the highest GPA. Maybe later in life it will be a raise or a promotion you want. There will be lots of examples as you move on in life. And they all have the same message. How can you expect it if you didn't work for it?"

"Good point," Brew said.

"And I guess you're right," Will said. "I didn't work for that award, so I'm definitely not going to win it."

"That's right," Harley said. "Just don't forget it. And don't forget to work for what you want. Because whether you work for something or don't work for something, either way you'll get what you deserve in return."

## CHAPTER FORTY ONE

"Come on, boys," Harley yelled from the truck the next week. "We're going back to the top of the hill one final time."

We all climbed in the back while David got in the front and then took the short drive back to the hill overlooking the river.

Harley sat down on his rock, then took a deep breath. "Well, this it," he said. "Our last meeting."

"Says who?" Will asked.

"Well, next week are your exams," Harley said, not that we needed reminding. "Then next weekend you graduate. So unless y'all plan on coming back from college next year, then I think this is our last meeting."

"I know," Brew said. "I have to admit, when you first asked us to meet with you every week, I didn't know what to think. Now I don't want it to end."

"Me either," David said.

"Well, that makes me feel good," Harley said. "And lucky for y'all, I've saved a really good one for last."

"I'm not surprised," I said.

"And you shouldn't be," Harley replied. "Here goes. I've been talking a lot this year about using your gifts, getting started, and not letting anybody tell you what you can't do. But instead, to hang out with people who tell you what you can do."

"Right," David said.

"But have you ever thought about the small difference between can and can't?" Harley asked.

"Not really," David replied.

"The only difference between can and can't, is a small apostrophe and the letter T," Harley said. "But just think how much that punctuation and one letter have kept people from doing."

He could probably tell from our stares and silence that we weren't quite following him. So he continued by asking us, "How do you spell can't?"

"C-A-N-T," Will said.

"And what does that stand for?" Harley asked.

"I'm afraid you're going to have to help us out," Brew said.

"I thought I might," Harley said. "C-A-N-T stands for *Creating A Negative Thought*. And it means just that. When you say that you can't do something, you're telling your mind that you can't do it. In other words, you're putting negative ideas in your noggin and creating a negative thought."

"I got it," Brew said.

"Now on the other hand, how do you spell can?" Harley asked us.

"C-A-N," I answered.

"Do you know what that stands for, or should I just go ahead and tell you?" Harley wanted to know.

"I'm guessing that the letter n stands for negative again," David said. "But other than that, I'm not sure."

"And you'd be almost right," Harley said. "Not negative, but negativity. C-A-N stands for *Chasing Away Negativity*. Just like saying that you can't do something is creating negativity, saying that you can do something is chasing away negativity. It's telling your mind to get rid of that negativity, so you CAN do whatever it is that you need to do. Make sense?"

"Definitely," Brew said. "You always have a good way of putting things into perspective."

"Thank you," Harley said. "I try. And I'll leave you with this to sum it all up. Use your gifts, don't put things off, don't stop, don't take life too seriously, and hang out with people that will lift you up instead of keeping you down. Now, go out there in life and make me proud."

I can't remember who did it first, and it doesn't matter. But as he stood up, we each stood up too. Not to leave, but to give him a standing ovation. He shook his head and smiled a little bit, probably thinking we'd lost our minds. He tipped his cap to us, then turned to walk away. He knew where his standing ovations in life, at least this one, were coming from.

## CHAPTER FORTY TWO

The following Friday was the last day of classes before exams started the next week. One of the classes I had was gym. It was the only class I had that year that neither David, Will or Brew was in with me. Mr. Daniels was our teacher. We played different games throughout the school year. During the winter we were always inside. But when the weather started to get warmer that spring, he took us out to play softball.

Upon arrival at the diamond he chose two guys at random and told them to pick teams. One of those two chose guys that he thought would actually be good softball players. The other chose guys that he liked, and thought would be fun to have on his side. I know that because I was one of the first ones he chose. Obviously, he didn't pick me because of my softball skills.

On that first day they beat the daylights out of us. I think it was twenty to nothing. Maybe not quite that bad, but close. The next day Mr. Daniels suggested that we choose new teams. But my team refused. We were convinced that the day before, the other guys had just gotten lucky and that today would be our time. We were wrong. They beat us twenty five to nothing. Again, probably an exaggeration, but not by much.

For the next several days Mr. Daniels kept suggesting that we choose up new teams, and every day we again refused. Finally, he stopped asking. Maybe he admired our determination, or maybe he just gave up trying to convince us how crazy we were.

They beat us every day for the next two months. Somedays it wasn't quite as bad as the first two days were. There were even a few times when we actually scored. But every day was embarrassing.

On that last day of classes, we had one more chance. We were determined that this would be the day. We played our hearts out and managed to hold them to only two runs, while we scored three. But they still had the bottom of the last inning to win. They got two outs and two hits. And like something out of an old movie, they had the tying run at third and the winning run at second, with their best hitter coming to the plate.

Playing out in left field every day was a guy named Craig. He was strong as an ox and made all conference in wrestling to prove it, but baseball was not his game. With a goofy sense of humor and loveable personality, Craig was the kind of guy everyone should have in their school.

Usually there were plenty of gloves to go around. But for some reason one was missing that day. So in the first inning Craig grabbed an orange cone like you see used on highway construction jobs. It was on the edge of the field and he said that he'd use that as his glove. We weren't about to argue. All we could do was hope the ball never came to him. Luckily it hadn't. Not at that point, anyway.

The other team's player who was at bat hit a high fly ball right out to Craig. It seemed to go in slow motion as we held our breath and watched it head toward him. He stood in position and held the cone over his head, I think he may have even had his eyes closed. The ball hit the corner of the cone, then bounced into the hole. Craig reached in, pulled the ball out, and held it up high.

Both teams looked over at Mr. Daniels who was standing halfway down the left field line serving as the umpire. He studied the situation for a second or two, scratched his chin, then threw his right thumb over his shoulder and yelled, "He's out!"

The entire team left their positions and ran out to left field to get Craig. He saw us coming and took off in the other direction. We caught him pretty easily and piled on top of him. Few teams that have won the World Series have ever been as excited.

About fifty yards away from the baseball field was a building of classrooms. We made so much commotion that several teachers and students walked outside to see what was going on. They probably never did find out. All they saw was a group of guys who, after two months of humiliation, finally had the bragging rights of fifth period gym class.

Later that night I was lying in bed thinking about that game. It reminded me of what Harley had taught us many times that year. To use your gifts and make the best of what you had. That day Craig only had a cone to use. But he made the best of what he had and won the game for us. Once again, Harley was right.

# CHAPTER FORTY THREE

The same week that we had our last week of classes, spring sports also ended. The lacrosse team did pretty well. Not as well as the basketball team, but better than the football team. Will had three hat tricks that year. Getting just one of those in a career is an accomplishment. To get three in one season is crazy. I guess his legs moved as fast as his mouth, so it was no surprise that he was awarded the MVP.

We got through exams the next week, and then on Saturday morning it was time for graduation. All the graduates and underclassmen wore the school uniform, only we had gowns over ours. As always, the ceremony was held on the lawn in front of the headmaster's house on top of the hill overlooking the river.

We marched in two by two, while our families who had made the trip stood for us. They all smiled and some even waved. But the last person I happened to see standing there was Harley. Looking very dapper in a navy blazer with a bow tie in the orange and blue school colors. It may have been the only time in my four years that I saw him outside when he wasn't wearing one of his Dowling caps, or at least holding one. He had a huge smile on his face as we made eye contact. I'm pretty sure he even slightly winked at me.

While most of the awards were given out at the actual awards ceremony, there was one that was so important it was presented at graduation. The Chaplain Award. The highest honor any student at Dowling could receive. It was the only award that wasn't earned in the classroom or in athletic competition. It was voted on by the administration, faculty and students and went to the student who was the nicest and most well liked by everybody.

While everyone who attended a homecoming, reunion or alumni event got a nametag with their senior picture on it, the winners of The Chaplain Award got a special nametag saying that they had won that award. When Mr. Phillips called Brewer's name as that year's winner, he seemed to be the only person in our class who was surprised.

After the ceremony, which included a commencement speech by an alum who had just been elected lieutenant governor of Delaware, there was a luncheon for everyone. Then our parents helped us finish packing and load our stuff in their cars. We'd all gotten into our first choice of colleges, but none were the same. Not even in the same states. Still, when we said our goodbyes, none of us made a big deal about it. It wasn't so much, "goodbye" as it was, "see ya."

# EPILOGUE

Fifteen years later, Will, David, Brewer and I returned to Dowling for the two hundred year anniversary. It was a weekend long celebration in the late fall that had several events including a football game against our arch rival. Hundreds of alums came from all over the country. Every hotel room within a fifty mile radius had been booked for months.

The four of us had seen each other at various moments since graduation, but this was only the second time that we'd all been together. The first being two years earlier when we all were in David's wedding. Just like Harley had predicted we would be.

David was the only one of us who was still as thin as they had been at graduation. Obviously running had continued to be a habit of his. He still had the dark blond curly hair, thought it wasn't as thick. After college he had gone on to med school, then became a pediatrician. His wife, who he met while doing his residency, was expecting their first baby in the spring.

Brew's dark hair now had a few premature sprinkles of gray. He had gone to work for his family's business, specializing in commercial real estate.

Will surprised us the most when he became a police officer after college. He was eventually promoted to detective. Then, just a few years later, he opened his own private investigation firm. Less than two weeks before our reunion, he became engaged to a gal from Mississippi. And, of course, he had asked the rest of us to be in the wedding.

As for me, after school I went to work for a production company. I learned the ropes and eventually decided to go out on my own and use my gift of storytelling as a documentary filmmaker. My first project was about battles of the Revolutionary War.

We caught up with each other as well as many other guys who had been at Dowling with us. We also caught up with the faculty members who had been around while we were there. Some who still worked at Dowling, others who had moved on but returned for the weekend. On the first night, as Mr. Phillips was making a speech welcoming everyone, he also announced that he would be retiring as headmaster at the end of that school year. On Saturday, after lunch but before the football game, we decided to go pay Harley a visit.

On the edge of campus, just next to the main entrance, is a very old church. An engraving above the door says that it was built in 1662. Some say it's the oldest church in Virginia. I've even heard it's one of the ten oldest in all of America. On part of the church grounds there is a small cemetery. There are people buried there who died in the late seventeenth century. We walked to the church and through that cemetery in silence until we found Harley's grave.

When he passed away three years earlier, all the alums were notified through the mail about a week later. None of us knew in time to attend his funeral, and this was the first time that any of us had seen where he was buried. Upon reading his tombstone we realized that he was older than we had thought. At the foot of the marker was one of his Dowling caps, along with a hammer that had also belonged to him weighing the cap down. Both had obviously been through all kinds of weather, but other than some rust on the hammer's head, they had held up pretty well.

"He certainly taught us a lot," a voice behind us said. We turned around to see four guys standing there. They looked to be about eight or nine years younger than we were.

"Excuse me, but what did you say?" Brew asked them before any of us had a chance to do the same thing.

"I was just saying that Harley taught us a lot," one of them said. "In our senior year."

"Wait," I said. "What do you mean exactly?"

One of the other guys in that group answered. "He used to meet with us every week and teach us life lessons."

"He did that for y'all too?" Will asked, just as surprised as the rest of us were.

"What do you mean y'all TOO?" one of them asked.

"He used to meet with us every week during our senior year," Will said. "And also taught us life lessons."

"No way," one of the other guys said. "Did he tell you that the word gift means, God is furnishing talent?"

"Yep," I answered. "He sure did."

One of the other younger boys spoke for the first time. "My personal favorite was that the word success stands for, something you can control every single second."

"I always liked those too," David said. "And I've tried to put them to good use over the years."

"I can't believe this," Brew said. "So you mean our group wasn't the only one that he taught those lessons to?"

"Hardly," a voice said. We all looked over and saw Mr. Phillips coming up to us. "I saw you gentlemen walking this way and thought this is where you might be headed," he continued.

"What did you mean by 'hardly'?" Will asked him.

"I meant you were hardly the only group he taught

those lessons to," Mr. Phillips answered. "Neither one of your groups were."

"We weren't?" David asked.

"No," Mr. Phillips replied. "Not even close. He did it every year. There were many years he met with more than one group. He just met with them on different days. You remember that time I said, 'I see you've been chosen this year,' don't you?"

"Yes, sir," Brew said. "I do remember that."

"Well, I had just seen you walking away from the hill and knew you were the ones Harley was meeting with that year," Mr. Phillips answered. "That's why I said you'd been chosen."

"You mean he just picked students at random each year?" one of the younger guys asked.

"He did," Mr. Phillips said.

"Come to think of it, Preacher said something about us being chosen too," I said. "Remember?"

"That's right, he did," David said.

"I don't know how he picked who he did," Mr. Phillips said. "But I do know the ones he picked were lucky. They probably learned more from him than they did in any classroom they sat in. Just don't go telling anybody I said that."

"I think I've heard that before," Will said.

"Come with me, gentlemen" Mr. Phillips said. "I want to show you something.

The eight of us followed him across campus to the hill overlooking the river. The same hill where we had met with Harley so many times in our final year at Dowling.

"Just stand here for a minute and take in that view," Mr. Phillips said. "I bet you've missed it."

We did just that, taking in the sweet Virginia breeze. After several seconds, Mr. Phillips continued. "Do you notice anything different about this area?" he asked.

We all looked around for several seconds before David finally yelled out, "Wait. What's that?" He was pointing to the rock where Harley always sat while he spoke to us. Then we noticed exactly what he was pointing to. On the rock was something that hadn't been there when we were students.

We walked over and took a closer look. There was a silver marker now attached to it. Engraved on that marker were the words, HARLEY'S ROCK.

"We had that put there right after he passed away," Mr. Phillips explained. "He touched the lives of so many students in his time here, we just thought it was fitting. And he also seemed to love this rock and this view."

"He did," we all said together.

"Alright," Mr. Phillips said looking at his watch, "It's almost time for the kickoff."

He turned to walk toward the football field and we followed him. Then we heard something overhead. We all looked up to see a flock of birds flying high in the sky, probably thirty of them, obviously heading south for the winter. And I couldn't help but notice that all those birds were using their gift. Not one of them was walking.

# About The Author

John Floyd is an award winning humorist and best-selling author. He first did stand-up comedy in a school talent show when he was only eight years old and has been using his "GIFT" ever since. Along the way he has shared the stage with Oscar, Emmy and Grammy winners. His previous books include *I'm The South* and *The Flower Lady*. He makes his home in North Carolina.

**www.johnfloyd.com**

# The Maintenance Man's Gift

## By John Floyd

*To The 700 Club, Thanks for everything you do!*

*God Bless,*

© 2020
All Rights Reserved

Some parts of this book are based on actual people, places and events. But other parts are fabricated in ways that only a southern humorist could think of.

You'll have to decide which is which.